SPRING INTO WINTER

a novel

by

Margot Grünewald Massey

WYMAN HOUSE PUBLICATIONS

Prepared and published by
WYMAN HOUSE PUBLICATIONS
360 Hilldale Drive, Ann Arbor, MI 48105-1119

Cover by Adrienne Kaplan, Ann Arbor, MI

Copyright © Margot Grünewald Massey, 1994
All rights reserved

LIBRARY OF CONGRESS
CATALOG CARD NUMBER : 94-061431
Massey, Margot Grünewald, 1926-
    Spring into winter.
    I. Title.

ISBN 0-925917-01-X

Printed in the United States of America by
BookCrafters, Inc., Chelsea, Michigan

Not to be reproduced in any way without written
permission of publisher. Very brief excerpts may be used
for reviews; please send copies to publisher.

This book is dedicated with love
to the memory of
Ida Weisskopf

SPRING INTO WINTER

- Chapter 1 -

"Oma," Inge Richter asked her grandmother, "did you know about Grete?"

Deliberately, Frau Landmann plucked a grape from the purple bunch in the dish on her bedside table, popped it into her mouth, and turned back to her granddaughter. She squashed the fruit with her gums and swallowed it, skin and seeds included.

"You mean that she has to go? Because of that silly edict?" The old lady's booming voice matched her Valkyrian frame.

"What edict? What's an edict? She told me that she was getting married."

Frau Landmann sighed gustily. "Poor girl!" she said, "I know. What else can she do? She has nowhere to go....An edict is a rule made by the government." She picked another grape and ate it. Then she lit a cigarette from the pack beside her, shook out the match and asked, "Did Grete tell you whom she was going to marry?"

"Oma, what edict are you talking about? The coalman, she said."

"What! The coalman!?" Frau Landmann snorted. "That scruffy *gannef*! A robber, always overcharges if I don't count the sacks!"

Frau Landmann commanded respect even without her dentures in place. She sat enthroned among the pillows of her bed, leaning back against the head-board. The green silk quilt that covered her legs was littered with the morning papers. Above her on the wall hung a large framed photograph of her deceased husband. He was portrayed lighting a cigar behind cupped hands, his face illuminated by the flame of the match; a walking stick dangled from his wrist by its crook.

Halfway down the old lady's nose clung horn-rimmed spectacles, and over them her intensely blue eyes twinkled at Inge. Her eyebrows were thick and white, her forehead broad, high, and ivory-smooth. A thin tail of braided white hair snaked over her right shoulder. She was wearing a lace-edged pink nightgown. Smoke from her cigarette curled up around her nose, and the ash was close to breaking off onto her majestic bosom. Just in time, Inge dashed for the ashtray on the bedside table. Frau Landmann ground out the stub.

"Thank you!" she boomed.

Inge stood back, pleating her skirt with her fingers.

"Well?" her grandmother said, "what about a good-morning kiss?" Actually, she said 'kith,' the lack of dentures impeding her speech.

Inge leaped onto the bed and buried her face in the loose flesh under the old lady's chin. Then she blew into it, making a sound like someone blowing bubbles under water.

"Steady! Steady, now!" Frau Landmann shook with laughter. This was their daily ritual and both loved it.

At the top of the thickly carpeted stairs that morning, Inge had hesitated. Should she walk down slowly, like a lady, and prolong the delicious agony of

Chapter 1

anticipation? Or should she use the banisters in her usual rapid giddy slide down the polished hardwood? Her grandmother had warned her a few days earlier not to expect a birthday party. The year 1938 was not a time for Jews in Germany to celebrate anything, she had said, let alone to have parties. Inge had to agree, outwardly. But it had always been a family tradition to pile the birthday gifts around the breakfast plate. So, no party, it couldn't be helped; there were sure to be presents, anyway. The thought of the gifts waiting for her made Inge decide to slide.

The day was already hot, and her hands squeaked on the banisters, braking her descent. Instead of arriving at the bottom with her usual flourish, she had to jump off clumsily. Scowling, she straightened her skirt. She pushed open the door to the *Wintergarten*, the conservatory where her place was set for breakfast.

One large, odd-shaped package, wrapped in pink tissue, lay on the table beside her plate. And a letter with a German stamp. Nothing from her parents, then? No brown-paper parcel from abroad? Not even a postcard with an exotic stamp? And what about Oma? Surely Oma can't have forgotten, too?

Disappointment made her swallow hard. Ignoring the pink package, Inge crossed to the bank of potted palms, ferns and cacti that grew in front of the picture window. Through blurred eyes, she looked at the hazy industrial valley of the Wupper, far below. She twisted off a piece of fern, rubbed it between her fingers and sniffed it absent-mindedly. Then she returned to the table.

SPRING INTO WINTER

At that moment, the door of the kitchen landing opened and Grete, the maid, walked in carrying the breakfast tray. Her broad face beamed above the milk and bread. When she saw Inge's disconsolate expression, she swiftly set down the tray.

"Many happy returns, my darling," she said and enfolded the girl in a warm embrace. "That's not a birthday face you are wearing, though!"

Inge breathed in the rose scent of Grete's soap mingled with the warm odors of kitchen and skin.

"There's nothing from my parents," she said, her voice quavering. "They've forgotten..."

"Of course they haven't forgotten," Grete said firmly. "Most likely there'll be something in the afternoon mail. You know that the mail from abroad is not reliable." She drew back her head and crossed her arms. A cascade of double chins descended towards the exposed triangle of red skin in the V of her cotton dress. 'Roast beef,' Inge had once called it. "Sit down and eat your breakfast. You'll feel better," she added.

Then she glanced at the unopened parcel and letter beside Inge's plate, and ruffled the child's short blond hair.

"You haven't even looked at your gift yet, nor opened your letter!"

Inge sat down and picked up the package. She fingered it, trying to guess its contents. It was soft, yet resilient.

"Go on! Open it!" Grete urged, standing over her.

"Who's it from?" Inge looked up. "Is it from you?"

Chapter 1

Grete nodded, blushing with pleasure. "I made it myself. Something to remember me by."

Inge ripped off the tissue and dropped it on the floor, where Grete retrieved it. Not looking at the child, she smoothed the crumpled paper carefully and waited.

Inge said nothing, just turned the curious object round and round, searching for an opening. It was heart-shaped, large as a head, and covered in bright pink satin. "INGE" was embroidered in yellow silk on one side, and on the other "FROM GRETE WITH LOVE".

"What is it?" she asked at last. "Where'd you open it?"

Grete looked hurt. She grabbed the thing and held it against her chest. Her eyes filled with tears.

"It's a cushion, can't you see?" she said. "I made it myself..."

Inge immediately jumped up, yanked the cushion from Grete's grasp, and threw her arms around the woman's middle.

"How silly of me," she mumbled into Grete's clothes. "Of course, it's a *cushion*! And...and it's *lovely*! Honestly!" She looked up, planted a quick kiss on Grete's soft white cheek and added, "Thank you very, very much. I...I just love it."

Grete loosened the child's arms and pushed her back into her chair. "All right, all right," she said gruffly. "I spent a lot of time on it, you know. Eat your breakfast now. And don't forget your letter. It's from your sister."

"Oh, it is, is it? So she did manage to send me a letter..." I suppose it was too much to have expected a present, she thought resentfully.

SPRING INTO WINTER

Inge bit into her buttered roll and said, crumbs flying from her mouth, "Don't you think it's mean of Erika not to send me a *present*? And what about Oma? Where's her present?"

"She's sure to have something wonderful for you," Grete said. "She probably wants to give it to you herself. But mind that you don't go and disturb her!"

Grete tucked the empty tray under her arm and turned to go. "Mind what I said, now," she added from the door, "you're not to disturb your grandmother before noon!"

"Oh all right! I'll go for a walk in the meantime."

Inge took another bite, glancing at the door that had just closed behind Grete.

Today was her tenth birthday, and not one member of her family was there to celebrate it with her! She felt overwhelmed by loneliness; the bread stuck in her throat.

Inge's family had been dispersed for nearly two years already. Her father, making a precarious living in exile, had been circling Germany from one country to another, unable to make a complete break and put either the ocean or another country between himself and his wife and children. Now, at last, he had settled in Belgium.

Inge's mother traveled back and forth between her husband and daughters. Erika, the eldest, was in Berlin with an aunt and uncle, to learn child care, and household duties in general. Inge herself had been left to the care of her maternal grandmother, Frau Landmann, in the large house near the forests of Northern Germany. The town of Wuppertal-Barmen lay snugly in a valley of the Bergische Land--the hilly country.

Chapter 1

Inge sniffled, and wiped her nose on the back of her hand. Not that she minded living with Oma, she reflected, far from it. She suspected that her parents would not have allowed her nearly so much freedom. But she would have liked to have been near her mother--so beautiful, always dressed so elegantly. And she smelled so good. In Oma's house, there were no scents to equal those. Oma disapproved of French perfume.

Inge picked up the letter and studied the envelope. "Fräulein Ingeborg Richter," it said. It was the first time anyone had called her "Fräulein." The few letters she had received until then, had been addressed simply to "Ingeborg Richter" or, more likely, to "Inge Richter."

Inge, impressed by her birthday importance, eagerly opened the letter.

"My dear little sister," Erika wrote. "Today is one of the most important days of your life. You are now ten years old. Never again will your age have only one digit. Happy birthday! Your loving sister Erika."

Loving sister indeed! How well Inge remembered being dragged screaming across the floor by that same loving sister. And once, having tied her securely onto the kitchen table, Erika had shaken pepper and salt into Inge's eyes, "to see the reaction," as the loving older sister had explained to their appalled parents upon their return.

Inge swallowed her milk angrily and nearly choked. She crammed another piece of roll into her mouth, then re-read the letter.

I suppose Erika means well, she thought. After all, two digits....I would never have thought of that. It struck

SPRING INTO WINTER

Inge that now, she was justified to consider herself grownup. Well, nearly grown up, anyway. Why, Erika's age, seventeen, had two digits. And so had her mother's, even Oma's. And I am the equal of them all, Inge gloated. Who knows, one day I might even have three digits. After all, some people lived to a hundred, or more. Look at those prophets, in the Bible. Some of them even begat at three digits, whatever 'begat' means. And she, Inge, was on her way there!

Considerably brightened by that prospect, Inge picked up the last piece of bread and Erika's letter, and left the house, cheerfully slamming the front door behind her with her foot. The weather was just right for a walk in the woods. The coolness under the trees would be lovely on this hot July day.

Few children now lived in the neighborhood. The owners of the large houses, like Inge's grandmother, were mostly parents of grown families. The children who did live there had been advised not to play with Inge, for fear of being branded "Jew lover." Consequently, Inge spent most of her time alone.

On the whole, however, she was content. There was plenty to do, much to read, and her active mind found an unending succession of scrapes to get into and pranks to play. She liked walking, and climbing trees. There were attics and cellars to explore, and disused sheds. Everywhere, she discovered long-forgotten treasures from her mother's childhood, from her aunt's and uncle's, even some from Oma's.

The forest lay on a hillside like a quilt sewn from different greens. The leaves of beech and oak, chestnut

Chapter 1

and birch shone golden in the morning sun. Behind a tangle of light trunks lurked the darkness of a pine grove. Little thrusts of wind along the ground scooped last year's leaves into an errant dance. There was the spicy scent of sun-dried fungi, a hint of pine cones, a foretaste of leaf fires to come. Birdsong here and there pricked shining holes into the pervading murmur of bees.

Inge settled herself among the roots of a favorite chestnut tree. They protruded to form a shallow basin. Munching the last of her bread, she spread Erika's letter on her drawn-up knees to read it again.

Ten years old. Soon to be grown up. Inge blew some crumbs off the paper, and the letter fluttered to the ground, exposing her knees. Inge gazed at them, fascinated. She had never really seen them before. There they were, ten-year-old knees, staring her bonily in the face. They were scratched, bruised, ingrained with dirt, shiny. They smelled like boys' knees, like her cousins' knees. Confused, Inge tried to drag her dress over them. Impossible! She jumped up, looked down at her legs--her dress only reached a few centimeters down her thighs. And she was ten years old!

Who *wants* to grow up? Inge thought. Growing up meant wearing longer dresses; longer dresses meant "good behavior." Good behavior meant no more tree-climbing, because girls weren't supposed to climb trees. It meant saying what was expected of you, not what you wanted to say. No! She would have none of it.

She flung herself full length onto the ground.

"I don't want two digits to my age," Inge decided. "Who cares about two digits? I want to stay nine!"

SPRING INTO WINTER

Feeling bereft of her single-digit years, she closed her eyes, rested her face on her arms and allowed her fingers to play blindly in the dirt. They encountered pebbles, and leaves papery from last autumn. Hollowed, blackened chestnuts, weightless as eggshells. Moss like velvet, and baby chestnuts.

Inge sat up and wiped away some unexpected tears, leaving a trail of dirt on her cheek. Picking up a handful of the hard green fruit, she let them trickle from palm to palm. They were no larger than a pea, and the same silvery green, their prickles soft as young grass. With a black-edged thumbnail, Inge split one open. Neatly embedded in even compartments of white flesh lay the embryo chestnuts, pearly and delicate. Defenseless. How easily they burst between finger and thumb! The survivors on the tree would grow to hard glossy auburn. In their ripeness, they would burst out of their protective barbed shell. They would bounce on the forest soil and lie forgotten in the grass, under leaves. Some animal might eat them, or some passing child gather them up to finger lovingly in a coat pocket. As I used to do, Inge thought. Some nuts would dig fat sturdy roots into the earth and grow into seedlings. Some would wither and shrivel, to become black bubbles of decay for years to come.

And so it would go on. Inge marveled at the soft immature nuts cradled in the nourishing flesh. Only last year, she had played with the unripe chestnuts that fell in their thousands from overburdened trees. Inge had thrown them in handfuls at her cousins. She had squashed them underfoot, enjoying their firm wet resistance. Yet she had never thought of splitting one open to study the

Chapter 1

inside. But then, she had been only nine, and the wonder of the world had been beyond her comprehension. From now on, things would be different.

As she walked home, a new awareness brought out details that Inge had never noticed before: golden dust-motes dancing in leaf-filtered shafts of sunlight; a column of ants marching in fluid file across her path, making a detour around a half-buried pebble.

Nearer home, the dust of sun-dry pavement prickled her nose. How uncared-for Oma's house looked, Inge thought. There were cracks in the white paint of the window frames, and the creeper needed trimming. The weed-grown front garden was delirious with bees. Only Grete's herb border, by the side of the house, was well-kept.

Inge skipped down the garden steps and walked into the kitchen through the back entrance. With her brand-new understanding, she was eager to show Grete her appreciation for the birthday gift. In all honesty, of course, she would have preferred something more useful, such as, for instance, a bag of liquorice candy.

Bursting into the kitchen, she called, "Grete! I want to..." Her voice trailed off awkwardly. "I want to... thank you..." She stopped.

Grete sat slumped at the kitchen table, her arms pushed up to the elbows into the potatoes she had been peeling for midday dinner. She was staring, unseeing, out of red-rimmed eyes.

"What's the matter?" Inge asked. Grete twitched, but did not reply.

SPRING INTO WINTER

"Grete, what is it?"

Inge had never seen her like this. Grete *always* smiled--at least when she was not scowling or telling Inge to get out of the kitchen. What could be wrong?

She put her arms around the woman's neck. Grete was breathing heavily, and a hairpin had worked its way out of her scant knot of mousy hair.

She turned a bleary face to Inge and said, "I'm getting married."

"Well! For heaven's sake!" Inge backed away. "You don't look very pleased about it!"

She was indignant. Grete had not even told her that she was "walking out." Underhanded, she thought it was. The least Grete could do if she was to get married-- and for the life of her, Inge could see no reason for it; wasn't this a good home?--the least she could do, was to be happy about it. People were supposed to be happy when they got married, weren't they?

Grete had pulled a handkerchief out of her apron pocket and was dabbing at her eyes. She forced her lips into a smile.

"Oh, I'm pleased all right," she said. Then, more firmly, as though to convince herself, "I'm happy. I really am happy!"

"Hmm!" Inge said. Curiosity however made her ask, "Who is it? Anyone I know?"

"Herr Nolle. You know, Alfred Nolle. He delivers the coal."

"That one! He's *old*!"

"No, he isn't. He is forty-six."

Chapter 1

"That's old." Inge was emphatic. "He's much too old for you. Besides, he's dirty."

"You watch out, miss!" Grete warned. "I won't have you insulting my man! And he's not too old for me. For your information, I happen to be...well...I'm forty-eight, myself." Inge was flabbergasted. "Besides," Grete went on, "he's not dirty on Sundays. And anyway, I don't see what business it is of yours."

She busied herself with the potatoes, viciously poking out their eyes.

"Oh, all right!" Inge said, huffed. "If that's how you feel about it, you can go and...you can go and damn-well marry your dirty old coalman!"

She shot out of the kitchen before Grete could reach out and slap her. She had forgotten all about thanking her for the cushion.

The realization of Grete's age was a shock. Grete had no right to any particular age. She must have been ten, once, Inge thought. She could not imagine Grete at ten. Did she have pigtails, perhaps, and wear wooden clogs, like little Dutch girls? But she was forty-eight now, and in a few years, she would be as old as Oma. No, that wasn't possible. Grete was ageless. She was there, she had always been there, always the same Grete, with her mousy hair, her white, rose-scented skin, and her triangle of "roast beef."

Inge tramped noisily up the stairs to the cloakroom, swearing under her breath. The very thought of Grete married was ridiculous. And to the coalman, yet!

She riffled a hand through the coats hanging in front of the wall-sized mirror. The brass rod responded musically to the shifting of the coathangers. Inge poked out her tongue at her reflection. She had to admit that she did not look anything like grown-up, in her short faded blue dress. Scruffy, she looked. She pinched her nipples. Flat as a plank. Thank heavens! Who wants breasts, anyway? They'd only get in the way when climbing trees.

From a scooped out underlip, Inge blew at the hair that had tumbled over her eyes.

She made a face as she passed in front of the portraits of her grandparents that were hanging above the massive fireplace in the hall. Sometimes she vaguely wished that they would punish her for all the times she had grimaced at them. But all they did, was to stare down at her with disapproval, watching her every move. Being naughty without the risk of retribution was only half the fun.

- Chapter 2 -

Inge had raced up the shallow green-carpeted stairs and paused on the landing, savoring the warm familiar scents of the big house. How she loved it! Even now, it retained the ghostly smell of its former prosperity. An expectant smile illuminating her face, Inge had hugged herself. What did Oma have for her?

Inge knew that her grandmother liked to read the newspapers in bed undisturbed, over a leisurely breakfast. But it was late, there was a gift to come yet, and Oma had never failed her.

Does Oma know about Grete? Inge wondered. Anyway, it was about time that she got up. It was nearly time for the midday meal.

Frau Landmann made no allusion to Inge's birthday, and Inge was not going to be the one to mention it first. Pretending unconcern, she vaulted over her grandmother and landed on her grandfather's bed, the twin of Oma's. It was always made up, though since Opa's death four years ago, it had not been slept in. Inge sprawled on her stomach on the quilt and propped her cheeks in her hands.

"Oma, the edict?"

Frau Landmann explained. Two years earlier, the German government had decreed that non-Jewish domestic servants up to the age of forty-five were to leave the Jewish households that employed them. Many of the women who lost their jobs as a result, had been absorbed into various industries, farm work, paramilitary, factories, and other occupations. Those for whom no employment could be found, became a charity problem for the government. But now, with the edict extended to all non-Jewish domestic servants in Jewish employ, the authorities were creating a situation hard to resolve. They were plunging into real hardship women who had, for all practical purposes, known no other homes than those of their Jewish employers. Many of them were too old to search for work elsewhere. The Nazi government found this yet another reason to blame the Jews for the economic straits in which Germany found herself.

"We've been lucky to keep Grete this long," Frau Landmann said. "Oh well, at any rate I am glad that she found a man to take care of her."

The old lady turned away, searching for her handkerchief. She trumpeted into it and wiped her eyes behind her glasses.

"Oh..." was all Inge could say. She sat up and hugged her knees.

"Take your shoes off the bed!"

Inge kicked them obediently onto the floor.

She could not imagine life without Grete. She had been told at some time that Grete had been in her grandmother's service for nearly thirty years. She had always been there, in the background of her own short life. She was there first when Inge came to visit her grandparents with her mother and father and sister. And this last year, when she had been living here for good, there was Grete, running her existence, seeing to her needs. For Inge,

Chapter 2

Grete was more representative of family life than her own parents.

"But she can't go, Oma! She can't leave us! What'll we do without her?"

The old lady shrugged, a tired shrug. "We'll manage, somehow," she said. "I've already started looking around for a nice Jewish girl."

Inge thought about the house without Grete. Would the warm cooking smells die out of the kitchen? Suddenly, she remembered the cushion Grete had given her, and her birthday.

"Oma," she said, bouncing excitedly up and down on the bed, "do you know what day it is today?"

Frau Landmann looked at Inge over her glasses, a twinkle in her eyes. "No-o-o," she said, "what day is it?"

"It's my birthday!" Puffing out her chest with pride, she added, "I'm ten years old today!"

Oma lay back into her pillows and folded her hands. "I had quite forgotten," she said blandly.

Inge knew very well that she was playing a game and, up to a point, was prepared to go along with it. But she had not received one single present yet--yes, the cushion, of course. As haughtily as she was able, Inge slid off her grandfather's bed.

"All right," she said, bending to tie her shoelaces. "I'll let you get up now. It's nearly dinnertime."

Squaring her shoulders, she marched towards the door without a backward glance. Wasn't Oma going to stop her?

"You come back here at once!" the old woman bellowed.

SPRING INTO SUMMER

Inge wheeled around, and there was Oma, her arms wide and laughing her toothless laugh. Inge leaped into them.

"Many happy returns, Inge," Oma said as she hugged and kissed her. A few hairs on her chin prickled Inge's cheek.

"Oma! You need a shave!" She giggled.

Frau Landmann slapped Inge's rear. "I'll teach you respect for your elders, you impertinent baggage!" she said, delighted. Inge nuzzled her happily.

"Here," Oma went on, rummaging in the drawer of her bedside table. "This is for you." She handed her a flat package, the size of a slab of chocolate. It was very heavy.

Inge fingered it, puzzled, then ripped off the tissue wrapping. Her face fell. She was holding a piece of smooth white-blond metal. "To my dearest Inge on her tenth birthday," was written on a card wrapped with it, "With all my love, Oma," And then the date.

Inge turned the metal over and over silently. She did not dare look up, because she was afraid that her disappointment would show.

Frau Landmann stroked Inge's hair with a heavy hand. "I know, I know," she said. "It isn't anything you expected. But..." and she intoned in her booming voice the saying that Inge had heard whenever anyone in the family received a seemingly worthless gift: "Not all that glitters is gold, nor is everything worthless, that looks like dirt!" Oma became serious. "Don't underrate this, Inge. It's a measure of security for your future."

Inge looked up at her grandmother's stern face.

Chapter 2

"What is it?" she asked, sniffling.

"It's platinum, and you are to keep it safe. Always."

Platinum. What good was platinum to a ten-year-old girl? A silly piece of metal. You couldn't eat it, couldn't play with it.

"Inge!" Frau Landmann's voice held a warning. "You are not to tell anyone--anyone!--that you have this thing! It's worth a great deal of money."

Inge felt doubly cheated. What if it was worth a great deal of money? she thought. Not only had Oma given her a useless present--well, at least of no immediate use--but, by its very value, she had imposed upon her the need for secrecy. Secrets were exciting only so long as you could impart them--in confidence--to someone else. And Inge could not think of anyone who would be remotely interested in a dumb piece of platinum.

Frau Landmann was watching Inge shrewdly.

"And just in case you would like a gift you can talk about," she said, "I have something else for you."

She groped under the pillows behind her and, after some mild cursing, found what she was looking for. On the flat of her hand she presented a rusty iron key, a twist of gray string knotted in its loop. Inge took it and weighed it on her palm. She looked up inquiringly.

"It's the key to the children's attic," Oma said. "Steady there! Take it easy!" she protested as Inge nearly choked the breath out of her. "Wait! After dinner, this afternoon, you may go up there and choose for yourself whatever you'd like." She lay back and sighed. "There now, child," she went on in a tired voice, "I see that has made you happier..."

SPRING INTO SUMMER

Inge was unable to speak. Despite much pleading, Oma had never allowed her access to the children's attic. It held the best-loved treasures of her mother's childhood, and of her aunt's and uncle's. Delight flowed warmly through her. Again she flung her arms around the old lady's neck and buried her face in the warm shoulder.

Frau Landmann pushed her away gently. She placed a finger under Inge's chin and studied her.

"Stop blubbering now!" she commanded. "Blow your nose and go wash your face. And tell Grete I'll be down in half an hour." She gave Inge a quick kiss, pinched her cheek, and added, "Be off with you, now!"

Inge hopped off the bed. As she reached the door, her grandmother called out, "I'll keep this for now," pointing to the slab of platinum forgotten on the quilt. "I'll put it in my safe until you...until we can leave the country."

Inge nodded, and smiled, and softly closed the bedroom door behind her.

From the marble shelf above the twin basins in the bathroom, Frau Landmann's teeth grinned at Inge in their glass of water. Her reflection in the mirror behind them grinned back at theirs. Her face was streaked with dirt. She opened full force one of the faucets. The water gushed out cold; there would be no hot water anyway.

In the spring of that year, Jews had been made to declare to the government any fortune above a ridiculous minimum, and that measure promised more stringent ones to come. Frau Landmann, to save fuel and money, had had a gas water heater installed above the sunken marble tub in

Chapter 2

the bathroom, so as not to have to feed the huge coal-burning water heater in the basement. But she had refused to go to the added expense of having it connected to the washbasins. Frau Landmann was afraid of a penniless old age. The old lady was living off her capital, but restrictive economical measures against Jews made themselves felt in every detail of daily life, and the capital was shrinking.

The thought of soon unlocking the children's attic, cast a glow of happiness over everything for Inge. With that certainty ahead, she could afford to wait a little. She felt mellow and generous.

"Beautiful, those teeth," she decided as she studied her grandmother's dentures, "*really* beautiful....Such workmanship!" she added aloud, imitating Oma's voice. It would be fun to take them out of the water, make them click and snap. She giggled as she pictured Oma's teeth independently biting the hand that fed them.

With growing anticipation, Inge could hardly wait to finish dinner. Frau Landmann was accustomed to eat in the oak-panelled dining room, and her granddaughter joined her there. The meal was silent as Inge, in her excitement, could not talk, and the old lady was lost in thoughts of her own. At last, the key clutched in a hot fist, Inge was free to climb the three flights of stairs to the attic.

The third floor and the stairs leading to it were reached by a door that separated it from the second. In former years, this part of the house had been the servants' quarters: two small and one large bedroom, and a bathroom. Since Frau Landmann's children had grown up and married, the maids had been moved to the room across from the master bedroom, on the second floor. Their former quarters had been turned into a self-contained apartment, and rented.

The Imhoffs, a childless Gentile couple, had lived there ever since Inge could remember. They were friendly, but kept to themselves. At Christmas, they joined the family around the tree. The Landmanns, like many assimilated Jews in Germany, celebrated Christmas as well as Chanukkah. And at Easter, the children--Inge, Erika and their cousins--climbed to the Imhoffs' apartment to collect Easter eggs.

Frau Landmann had kept the right of passage, since the attic above the Imhoffs' apartment held the wash-kitchen with its copper boiler and stone trough, as well as the spacious drying area under the rafters.

The attic ran the whole width of the house and was kept spotless. On the weekly washday, Grete hung the wash to dry there, unless the weather was sunny and then, she spread the sheets on the lawn behind the house. Dormer windows in the sloping roof admitted daylight to all but the farthest nooks and corners. The room smelled warmly of dry wood, resinous and clean.

On the left, next to the top of the stairs, in an angled corner closed off by a slatted fence and secured with a padlocked gate, was the children's attic. Not even Grete had been allowed access to clean it. Inge had often stood there, pressing her nose greedily through the wooden slats. She could only dream longingly into the gloom, barely making out the tempting shapes: a rocking horse,

Chapter 2

a doll's buggy on grotesquely high wheels, a domed chest in the angle of roof and floor, and baskets of dolls and stuffed toy animals. Frau Landmann had jealously forbidden her grandchildren to forage there--it was sacred ground. And now she, Inge, was to unlock the treasure!

The lock was stiff, and the rust on the key did not help. Inge was clumsy in her eagerness. At last, with a pained squawk, the lock sprung open. Her breath short and shallow, Inge unhooked the latch.

As in a dream, she gave the horse's tailless rump a shove, and it rocked silently on a bed of dust. Its nostrils still flared bright red, its eyes were bloodshot. Dust slid gently from its smooth painted back. The once-black mane, when Inge caressed it, disintegrated at her touch.

Here and there, a glass eye stared from a tangle of toys in a wicker basket. Inge pulled at a brown tail and cleared a near-lifesized monkey from the heap. It leered at her from under heavy felt lids, a wide felt smile splitting its face. Inge shook it gently, and a cloud of dust surrounded her. She dropped the monkey back into the basket and wiped her hands on her dress.

She stumbled against a large box and lifted its lid. Inside, neatly ranged, she found a collection of stone building blocks--bridges, half bridges, fractions of arches. There were round columns, roof blocks, window frames. The stones were smooth with a long-gone boy's dirt rubbed into their pores.

At her touch, the doll's buggy creaked on wheezy springs. Inge leaned over it, sniffing the odor of ancient oilcloth. The inside was upholstered in once-white padding, now dirty ivory. A stiff blanket concealed a long lumpy shape. Inge peeled it back, and dust poured onto her dress and shoes. Under the cover that had kept it clean, lay the most beautiful doll she had ever seen.

Inge had never cared for dolls, preferring more active pursuits. Once, when she had been given one, she had disemboweled it to remove the 'mama' voice box, to keep in her pocket. She had carefully twisted off its head to study the inside, and how the eyes closed and opened. Then she had buried the remains in a corner of the garden.

But this was something else, something more than a mere doll. This was a creation, a work of art. Inge lifted it reverently from the buggy. It looked fresh and new.

The doll was as long as Inge's arm, the limbs and head made of porcelain delicately tinted, and the gently curling auburn hair looked real. The eyes, when she lifted it, opened upon deep blue irises. Real lashes seemed to grow from the moving china lids. Through rosy half-open lips peeked two pearly teeth. The arms and legs were articulated at the joints, even at ankles and wrists. The doll was dressed in a purple silk gown with tiers, yellowed lace at neck and elbows. The silk whispered sibilantly when Inge ran her finger gently across it. She lifted the heavy skirt to inspect the underthings: lacy bloomers ended in gathers below the knees.

Inge hugged the doll in a sudden spurt of love. This was what she wanted, what she had always wanted, though she had not known it! This was her choice. Tenderly, she carried the doll downstairs, to show Oma.

When Frau Landmann saw Inge with the doll in her arms, she pushed herself slowly up from her armchair. Her eyes widened, and she touched the string of pearls at

Chapter 2

her neck.

"That's Amalia's doll," she whispered, sinking back into her seat. "I had forgotten it..."

"Who is Amalia?" Inge asked. She felt guilty, as if she had trespassed and been caught in the act. Gently she placed the doll in her grandmother's lap. "Shall I put it back?"

The old lady's thick fingers stroked the doll's hair. "Amalia..." she murmured, "Amalia..." Two tears rolled slowly down her wrinkled cheeks. Inge backed away with a heavy heart.

"Don't go, child," Frau Landmann said. "You couldn't have known..." Then, still caressing the doll, she added: "Amalia was my first-born. She died, when she was five. She was...so sweet." The old lady fell silent. Then, smiling a little, she said, "But then, one year later, your mother was born. So..."

Inge ached with her grandmother's grief. "Let me put the doll back, Oma," she said.

"No, child. You should keep her; it's right. I am happy you chose her. Take her." She held the doll out to Inge on hands that shook slightly.

Inge carried it back to her room. She sat it up against the pillow on her bed and, lying on her stomach in front of it, stared long into the unblinking blue eyes. Eyes that had last stared back at a little girl named Amalia--such a funny old-fashioned name--dead now so many years. Inge felt as though she was looking straight back into last century. With sudden clarity she recognized, as a tangible truth, her own link with the past.

"Your name will be 'Amalia'," she said to the doll.

- Chapter 3 -

The summer vacation was drawing to a close, and the authorities were prodding Grete to leave the Jewish household. The last night she was to spend in her old room, she allowed Inge to stay with her.

Sleeping in Grete's room had always been a special treat. There was a second bed, from the time when there had been two maidservants. Inge loved to watch Grete prepare for bed. Grete was extremely modest, and to humor her, Inge pretended to close her eyes; however, she peeked.

She watched as Grete slipped her ample white nightgown tentlike over her head, and undressed underneath it. Inge wondered if she did that also when she was alone in her room. The nightgown looked comically alive as Grete fought her way out of her clothes. Finally, her head emerged, disheveled, her face flushed with effort and temper. Around her feet lay a crumpled heap of pink and white.

"Grete?"

"Didn't I tell you to keep your eyes shut?" said Grete in a cross voice.

"But they are closed! Look!" Inge squeezed her lids tightly together and grinned.

Grete smiled reluctantly. "Go on with you," she said. "Go to sleep. It's late."

"I can't sleep."

She sat up and hugged her knees, and watched as

Chapter 3

Grete took the pins out of her hair and shook it loose over her shoulders. It was thin and straggly. Grete then took a brush in one hand and a heavy comb in the other--much too heavy for that poor crop, Inge thought--and dragged them alternately through her hair, furiously, over and over. She seemed to be releasing on her hair all the frustrations of her life.

And then came the part that Inge had been waiting for: with the teeth of the comb, Grete raked through the bristles of the brush, harvesting a woolly ball of light brown fluff. This she pushed into a white cone-shaped celluloid container that was hanging beside the mirror above the washbasin.

"What do you *do* with your hair?" Inge asked. It had been a mystery for a long time, and this was her last chance to find out.

"Do? Why, I throw it out!" Grete turned an astonished face toward Inge. "What on earth should I do with it?"

Inge lifted her shoulder. "Oh, I don't know," she said. "It seems such a waste..." She giggled, adding, "You could stuff cushions with it! When you've collected enough, I mean....Maybe you stuffed *my* cushion with it?"

Grete laughed, blushing. "You do have the craziest ideas! I'll miss you..." She cleared her throat, then went on with forced cheerfulness, "Maybe I could weave a hairshirt with it, and wear it for penance!"

Inge knew that Grete was Catholic. From her, she had learned many of the rituals of that religion.

"Have you done something bad?" she asked.

SPRING INTO WINTER

Grete did not reply. She turned back to the mirror and braided her hair for the night, one thin tail, like Oma's. Only it was brown. Then she brushed her teeth, and gargled at length.

"Well? Did you?" Inge insisted.

"Did I what?"

"Do something bad."

"Of course not. I have nothing to reproach myself for. Go to sleep and don't bother me."

Grete peeled back her sleeves above the elbows and soaped her face, neck and arms. The peppermint scent of her toothpaste mingled with the rose of her soap.

"Grete?"

"What is it *now*?"

"When are you getting married?"

"Saturday. Day after tomorrow."

"So soon....Will you have a long white dress and a veil?"

Grete shook her head. "Unh-hunh," she said, "just my Sunday best."

"Will you get married in church? Can I come?"

"No. No, I'm not getting married in church, Albert isn't Catholic. And you can't come, sweetie, I'm sorry. Nor your Oma, either..." Grete's eyes filled with tears. "I would have loved you both to be there, but..."

Inge sucked the knuckle of her thumb. She did not ask any more questions. The bed beside hers creaked as Grete sat on its edge. She reached up and yanked the lightpull that dangled above the brass bedhead. The room plunged into night and immediately, like a theater backdrop, the window sprang to bright blue life.

Chapter 3

Night had not yet fully fallen; summer evenings were long. The curtains remained undrawn and little by little, white stars appeared. Grete's room was at the back of the house, overlooking the valley. When lying in bed, the windows framed nothing but sky.

Grete's voice came muffled from Inge's left. "You won't miss much," she said. "It's only going to be a civil wedding, at the registry office. Besides..." She fell silent.

"Besides what?" Inge prompted.

"Oh, nothing."

In her mind's eye, Inge saw Grete's lips tighten to a thin line. "Come on! Besides what?"

"Oh, Inge...I don't agree with him, with Herr Nolle! Not on this, I don't! You know I don't hold with this nonsense against you Jews!"

Inge felt her stomach contract. In a clear thin voice, she said, "You mean that Herr Nolle doesn't...doesn't like..." She swallowed, unable to go on.

"No, he doesn't like Jews," Grete said. She rolled over the separation between the two beds and gathered Inge up in her arms. "My poor sweetie, my little child," she crooned into her hair.

Inge let herself go against Grete's warm body. It was such a safe place, so comforting when one was hurt.

"If I could change this nasty world..." Grete murmured. "Oh, Inge, if only your mother were here, to take you away..."

Inge stiffened. Her mother was never there, and now Grete too was to be taken away. The unfairness overwhelmed her. It also awakened her pride, and a vaguely sensed promise of self-reliance. Gently, she freed herself, and Grete returned to her own bed.

"Never mind, Grete," Inge said in a tight voice, "I understand. I know how it is."

She lay in the narrow white bed and stared blindly at the ceiling. At the first glimmer of dawn, she rose silently and looked down at the sleeping Grete. Her face was puffed and an unhealthy white. Inge had heard her weep softly, long into the night. Bending closer, she noticed for the first time wrinkles on Grete's forehead, under her eyes, from nose to mouth. She put out a hand as though to smooth them away, but withdrew it before she had touched the woman. She could not bear the thought of saying good-bye.

Stealthily, Inge left the room and returned to her own to get dressed. She went down the stairs on tiptoes. The house was deeply still, and the gray dawn had made everything the color of death.

In the kitchen, Inge broke off a piece of stale bread. Nibbling it, she let herself out of the house into the morning stillness.

The garden was wet with dew and smelled of fresh laundry. Inge breathed deeply, filling her lungs with the moist air. She walked into the early-morning woods and listened to the birds waking one another, till the air sparkled and dripped with song.

When at last, hours later, she returned to the house, Grete had gone. She had removed all trace of herself from her room, even the hairtidy. Only the scent of rose soap lingered faintly in the air.

Chapter 3

Inge saw how Grete's departure made Frau Landmann realize how much they both had relied on her, to what extent she had smoothed their life. Grete had been Oma's right arm, the crutch that was knocked from an invalid's grasp. A young Jewish girl was to replace her soon, but could anyone take Grete's place? Until her arrival, the old lady and Inge would have to fend for themselves.

At her grandmother's direction, Inge learned to scrub the kitchen floor, while the old lady slowly pushed the massive Hoover over the Oriental rugs. The child learned to prepare breakfast, and to carry it upstairs: coffee, milk for herself, bread and a dot of butter, cheese, sausage, and raspberry jam. She would set the tray down on her grandmother's bed and they would eat together, in silence. Frau Landmann dunked her bread in the coffee, to soften it. Afterwards, Inge took the tray downstairs again to the kitchen and washed the dishes in water heated on the gas stove. While she washed up, she gazed out of the semi-basement window at Grete's herb garden, just level with her eyes.

The mint was spreading and weeds had started to grow among the thyme and parsley. The chives grew purple flower heads and no one bothered to crop them.

One day, a little brown dog came trotting down the garden steps, sniffed at the herbs, then lifted his leg against the window frame. When Inge banged on the glass, he turned towards her an idiotically grinning face, wagged his curly tail, turned around and with his hind legs, scraped a patter of dirt like hail against the window pane.

SPRING INTO WINTER

It became Inge's duty to go down the hill to shop for groceries. The first time, she went by bicycle, free-wheeling down the curving road. It would mean pushing the bike uphill all the way home, but that way, she would be able to carry more and save herself another trip. She would tie the purchases onto the baggage carrier behind the seat.

The stores where Frau Landmann had shopped for well over forty years lined one side of the street--once the village main street--halfway down the long hill. Further up, a couple of cows grazed in a field, and a horse or two. Halfway between the village street and the prosperous suburb higher up the hill where Frau Landmann lived, was a farmhouse, walls and roof clothed in slate tiles.

Inge knew the stores well. She had often accompanied Grete on her shopping expeditions, and, once in a while, Frau Landmann herself. On those occasions, there had always been some friendly banter between the shopkeepers and Grete, and some goodie or other for Inge. When she had gone with her grandmother, the merchants had been respectful but friendly towards the old lady, and indulgent toward Inge; she still received a candy, or an apple, or, from the butcher, a chunk of sausage. Inge had never noticed any unfriendliness. Her first stop today was the butcher's shop.

Frau Landmann had telephoned her order, and Inge only had to pick it up. Like all the other shops, this one now displayed a sign in its window, proclaiming that "This is a German Shop".

Chapter 3

Inge leaned her bicycle against the stone wall by the door, careful not to bump the display window. She could see Herr Fritsche watching her from behind the counter, red hands resting on ample hips clad in a bloody white apron. Inge liked Herr Fritsche.

When she entered the shop, the butcher's wife, who sometimes helped her husband, snorted, and said loudly, "Ah! The Jew brat!" With this, she flounced out the back door.

Inge blushed, not knowing how to respond. Should she turn around and leave? But Herr Fritsche winked at her.

"Never you mind her," he said, jerking his head in the direction of his vanished wife.

Inge tried to smile. "I come for my grandmother's order," she said.

"That's right. And I got it ready for you, too, and a nicer little knuckle of veal you couldn't wish for. No, sir!" Herr Fritsche wiped his hands on his apron and reached under the counter.

As he bent over, Inge saw his scalp flush under the yellow hair, and the rolls of fat at the back of his neck become thicker. Puffing, he brought out a white paper parcel tied with string.

"There you are! The nicest little knuckle of veal you could wish for," he repeated. "You let me know if your Oma isn't pleased with it. You just tell me!"

Again Herr Fritsche winked. "Your Oma has been my best customer for God knows how long, *and* my father's before me. And don't let anyone tell you different!"

Embarrassed, Inge shifted her weight from one foot to the other and smiled. She waited for her sausage.

SPRING INTO WINTER

"Here you are, then! And here's a little something for you too," Herr Fritsche said. He selected a long slim knife from the row behind his well-worn butcher's block. With a flourish, he sliced a large chunk from one of the sausages hanging in bunches from the ceiling. He impaled it on the point of the knife and held it out to Inge. She took it, looking apprehensively towards the back door.

"Thank you very much," she said, and automatically performed the little curtsy that she had been taught in early childhood, as good manners demanded.

"Never you mind *her*," Herr Fritsche whispered, with a conspiratorial look over his shoulder. "She'd better not try any nonsense with me, she'd better not. I can handle her, that I can!"

"Wer*ner*!" Frau Fritsche shrilled from the back. "Haven't you done yet with that Jew brat? There's orders to be filled!"

"Yes, *Liebchen*, right away!" Defiantly, the butcher sliced off an even larger chunk of sausage and threw it at Inge. She caught it deftly and laughed.

"Thank you, Herr Fritsche," she said as she left the shop.

"Heil Hitler!" the butcher called after her, cheerfully, and winked once more.

Inge tied the parcel of meat onto the baggage carrier and pushed the bike along to the druggist's. She was to get a tube of toothpaste, two cakes of toilet soap, and some soft green soap for the laundry. Inge and her grandmother were going to do the weekly wash.

Inge loved this shop. It smelled warm and spicy. Buckets and brooms hung from walls and ceilings. Jostl-

Chapter 3

ing each other on the well-worn wooden counter were glass jars of cough drops, sour drops, licorice roots, bay leaves and cloves. Packets of different brands of soap powder were stacked on the floor. There were herbs in wooden, lead-lined drawers, chamomile tea, senna pods. Drums of scouring powder, bundles of dishcloths.

Three stone steps led up into the old store, an iron railing flanking the right side. Inge leaned her bicycle against it.

A bell was set tinkling as she pushed open the door. At the sound, a loud "Heil Hitler!" issued from behind a stack of boxes, then the caller of the greeting followed.

"Oh, it's you!" the woman said. Frau Hornreich looked as though vinegar might be her favorite tipple. She was pale and stringy, and her eyes closely hugged her sharp nose.

"Good morning, Frau Hornreich," Inge said, "I would like..."

"Didn't you hear me say 'Heil Hitler'?" Frau Hornreich interrupted.

"Yes, but..." Inge blushed.

"Well? What are you waiting for?"

"But...I...You know..." Inge wondered at the sudden hostility. Frau Hornreich had never been particularly friendly, but neither had she been openly hostile. Perhaps she wasn't feeling well? She didn't look too healthy, pale as she was.

"This is a German shop," Frau Hornreich said, "or can't you read? Jews are not welcome!" She pushed her face close to Inge's and snarled, "In a German shop, the greeting is 'Heil Hitler,' and don't you forget it!" She

SPRING INTO WINTER

straightened up and planted her hands on her hips.

Inge swallowed. Half-heartedly she lifted her right arm in the Nazi salute and mumbled, "Heil Hitler."

"Louder!" Frau Hornreich commanded, "so I can hear it!"

"Heil Hitler!" Inge shouted, head high, her cheeks flaming. Her blue eyes blazed at the woman. "And now, my order! Please," she added, as an after-thought.

Frau Hornreich leaned over the counter. "Got the cash?"

"But....My grandmother pays by the month. Doesn't she?"

"Not anymore, she doesn't! From now on, it's cash on the dot, from Jews. You tell the old witch up on the hill!"

Inge clenched her fists. The shopkeeper had never spoken like this in Grete's presence. Inge felt like spitting into the spiteful face. This used to be such a wonderful place, its exotic odors conjuring up far-flung dreams. What had happened? She turned away. If only Grete were there....Inge realized how much Grete's presence had protected her.

"Heil Hitler!" Frau Hornreich screeched again as Inge left the shop to the tinkle of the bell.

She closed the door behind her, and wheeled the bicycle to the greengrocer's. Out of the corner of her eyes, she noticed a group of boys on the other side of the street, snickering as they looked at her.

Some women in the shop stood talking together with animation, their purchases in baskets at their feet. When they saw Inge, they fell silent and turned their backs to her. Then they resumed their conversation. The

Chapter 3

greengrocer came in from the back, and Inge went over to him where he stood by the hanging scales.

She bought a pound of peas, rather old and dry ones. Then carrots, beans, and onions. She was glad that Oma's cellar held plenty of potatoes. At least she would not have to lug those.

"Onions!" one of the women said to the other, snickering. "You hear that? She wants onions! Jews *live* on onions. It's a fact!" They all laughed.

"Put it on the bill, please, Herr Schmidt," Inge said, ignoring the women.

Herr Schmidt took a stub of pencil from behind his ear, licked the point, and made a note on a sheaf of bills hanging on the wall, spiked on nails.

"You tell your grandma that from now on, she'll have to pay cash," he said. The women smirked. Herr Schmidt shrugged and showed his palms. "I'm sorry, Inge," he said, "but that's the way it's got to be from now on. To be on the safe side, you understand."

"I'll tell my grandmother," Inge said, blushing, and left the store.

She secured her purchases on the baggage carrier.

"Dirty Jew, dirty Jew,

Eating only onion stew!"

the boys chanted from the other side of the street.

Inge ignored them. It was not the first time that she had heard that ditty. Then she noticed that both the tires were flat. She leaned the bicycle back against the wall and examined the damage. The tires were studded with brass thumb tacks.

SPRING INTO WINTER

Her first thought was that one would have done just as well. Why use so many? Then fury flooded her in a white-hot torrent. She straightened up, breathless. The boys across the street were hopping up and down with glee, howling with laughter.

Inge never knew how she crossed that street. She found herself hurtling into the bunch of boys, hitting out at the evil grinning faces as hard and fast as she could. She had lost all feeling beyond the lust to hit out, to hurt. It was as though a dam had broken, a dam that until now had prudently held back her urge to retaliate.

Unfair! Unfair! hammered in her brain. She did not feel the boys kick back at her, tear her hair and clothes, rake dirty fingernails across her cheeks. There were three of them, but Inge had the strength of her rage. She dealt bloody noses and black eyes.

An iron fist yanked her from the battling knot of children. She was held panting at arm's length by a huge black-haired woman who smelled of laundry soap and sweat. Her red face was contorted with hatred.

The woman held Inge with one hand, and first with the palm, then with the back of the other, slapped her face, hard.

"I'll teach you!" she screeched as she hit out again and again. "Dirty Jew brat! I saw you! Attack good Aryan boys, would you? Take this! And this! And that! Scum! Jew!"

The boys danced around the two, jeering and hooting. At last, the woman dropped Inge, wiped her hands on her blue apron and, turning angrily on the boys, shooed them away.

Chapter 3

Inge dragged herself over to her bicycle and slowly, carefully, started to push it up the hill. It was made heavier by the groceries that the boys had not touched. The flat tires bumped on the gravelly road. Inge's arms ached. She licked her lips and tasted blood. Her left eye was closed. Her dress was torn, and her knees shook; she fought against dry, nervous sobs.

The cowards! Unfair! Inge refused to cry.

She hated the entire world. She hated Oma for making her go to the stores. She hated Frau Hornreich, and the women at the greengrocer's, and those smelly, beastly boys, and that big woman who had slapped her. Bitterly she hated Grete for abandoning her. It's all your fault, Grete! Inge thought. You knuckled under, and I despise you.

As she neared home, her overriding thought was to avoid her grandmother. She wanted to remove the traces of her battle before facing the old lady.

- Chapter 4 -

But Frau Landmann was waiting on her look-out bench. The old lady was resting from her unaccustomed chores. The bench was built into an alcove on the porch that ran from the corner of the house down the side to the front door, and overlooked both the street and the house next door. Before that house was built, about twenty years earlier, the bench had looked out over part of the valley as well.

Inge tried to push past her grandmother, pretending not to see her sitting there in the shade. But Frau Landmann shot out her walking stick and hooked Inge's arm with its crook. Inge came to a sudden stop.

"What in the name of heaven have you done to yourself?" Frau Landmann demanded.

Inge studied her shoes and kicked the floor. How was she to explain the fight and its reason?

Inge had not been taught to be proud of her Jewishness, nor to make excuses for it. She was Jewish, and that was that. It seemed that her grandmother felt that she had no right to preach ethnic pride or religious righteousness. Frau Landmann knew that in Germany at this time, those sentiments could only lead to trouble, to persecution. She did not wish to make a martyr of Inge, who had been left in her care, and whom she meant to restore her to her parents healthy in mind and body.

Chapter 4

Inge, however, chafed against those restrictions she felt were imposed upon her by the Nazis. She did not think that being Jewish made her in any way different from other children, and resented the unfairness of their treatment of her. But she was unable to put this into words.

"If I've told you once, I have told you a hundred times: do *not* race your bicycle down that hill!" Frau Landmann said. "But will you listen? No, not you, Miss High-and-Mighty!"

"But Oma, I didn't..."

"Tush! Don't try to wriggle out of it! It serves you right, and don't expect any sympathy from me!"

"I did *not* fall!"

"Don't you yell at me! I'm not deaf!" Frau Landmann roared. Then, as Inge's statement sank in, she said, "*What* did you say? How *did* you get into this state?"

"I had a fight. With some boys."

"Ladies don't fight," Frau Landmann said primly. "Fight? Whose boys?"

"Damn it all, how should I know whose boys. Some boys on the Hochstrasse. I don't know them."

"Don't swear. And if you must fight, at least fight with someone you know!"

"They knew who I was, anyway. They called me names. Jew, and so on. And they punctured my tires. So I got mad. So I fought them."

"Did you hurt them? How many were there?"

"Three." Inge wiped her nose, and the friction broke the crust that had started to form on her split upper lip. "I want to go and wash. The shopping's on the bike." She started to move off, then stopped. "Yes, I think I did hurt them. A little, anyway."

"*My* girl!" Frau Landmann said proudly. "My girl fights three boys and beats them up singlehanded!"

Inge, who had been on her way in, stopped and wheeled around. "I did not beat them up," she said. "They beat me up. They, and a fat smelly woman. And I won't go shopping again, ever! I don't care if we starve! I am not going down that hill again, and you can't make me!"

She burst into tears and rushed into the foyer washroom, where she splashed the basin with water and tears mixed with dirt and blood.

Inge spent part of the afternoon trying to repair the damage to her bicycle. She pried the tires off the frames with the handles of kitchen forks and hauled out the inner tubes. Then she found that they were beyond repair. There were just too many punctures.

After a few days, of course, Inge had to swallow her pride and fear, and go down the hill again. Frau Landmann could not walk that far, nor carry the heavy loads, and the merchants refused to make deliveries now. There was no other way to get supplies. Inge had to go shopping nearly every day, since she was able to carry only limited loads. She had been unable to find new inner tubes for her bicycle. Nor would she have used it, if she could.

As she passed the slate farmhouse on one of her trips down, a girl about her own age stepped out of the door and, smiling, came up to Inge.

Chapter 4

Inge was about to pass her when the girl said "Hello!"

"Hello," Inge replied, embarrassed, and stopped.

"You live up at the big house, don't you? I've seen you."

Inge nodded. She was by now afraid that whoever addressed her, would abuse her. Every stranger was a potential enemy. Yet she too had noticed the girl. However, since she was not of Frau Landmann's circle of acquaintances, Inge had not had the opportunity to meet her 'officially'. The old lady kept a firm hand on Inge's social life, such as it was. Inge was pleasantly surprised by the friendly 'hello'--usually, these days, it was 'Heil Hitler!'.

"What's your name?" the girl asked. "Mine's Elfriede."

"Inge." Blushing, defiant, she added, "You don't have to talk to me. I'm Jewish."

Elfriede tossed her head. "I know you're Jewish. Everybody knows. Who cares? My Dad doesn't!"

Inge smiled at Elfriede with guarded relief, and looked at her curiously. The girl was skinny and pale, with yellow hair in ringlets. She wore thin gold loops in her ears, her gums showed when she smiled, and her teeth were very bad. Her dress, pink with frills, was too long.

The two girls stood facing each other, grinning and shifting from foot to foot.

"Well," Inge said at last, "I've got to be going. I have to go shopping. 'Bye, for now!"

"I'll come along," Elfriede said, and fell in step beside her. She smelled of boiled vegetables.

SPRING INTO WINTER

"Oh, but you mustn't! There're boys who....Your mother might not want you to. Go ask your mother!"

"My Mom doesn't care. She's on the bottle." Inge wondered what that meant. Babies were on bottles, that she knew. But a mother? Elfriede grabbed Inge's hand and said, "Boys don't scare me. I've got a big brother. Come on!"

She started swinging Inge's arm, and soon, the two were skipping down the hill together, laughing as they went. Frau Landmann's black leather shopping bag, limp with age, was slapping gaily against Inge's calf.

In the dairy, a customer said to Elfriede, "Aren't you ashamed of yourself, going with a Jew? I'll tell your mom on you, I will!"

For answer, Elfriede stuck out her tongue and made a rude noise. Inge giggled nervously. It was a long time since she had thought anything so funny. The woman shook her fist near Inge's face, not quite touching it, swore at the other girl, and slammed out the door. The other errands were accomplished without incident, though a few shopkeepers and their customers made remarks to Elfriede--which she ignored--and raised disapproving eyebrows.

When Inge left her new friend near the farmhouse, it was with a feeling of excitement, a new expectancy. If a girl had a friend, a real friend, nothing was impossible.

Bubbling with high spirits, she returned home and, dancing circles around her grandmother, told her about her new acquaintance, someone with whom she could play and who moreover was a close neighbor. "And Oma, her ears are pierced," she added, "and she has real gold

Chapter 4

earrings in them!"

"Obviously, low-class persons," Frau Landmann said coldly. Inge's spirits sank. "Where did you say she lives?" her grandmother continued. "*We* do not allow our children to wear earrings."

"But it's pretty!" Inge protested. "And she lives in the slate house."

"Oh. The slate house. Not our kind of people at all. I thought as much. The slate house, indeed!"

"Why? What's wrong with them?"

"Those people are notorious! I do not wish you to associate with them."

"Why? What have they done?"

"I do not wish to discuss it. It is well known that the woman drinks." So *that's* the bottle, Inge thought.

"But Elfriede is a *nice* girl! And no one else wants to play with me, anyway." Inge's underlip jutted defiantly.

"I'll ask Frau Grünberg to come over with her granddaughter, tomorrow. You can play with her. She's your own age, too."

"I don't want to see her! I can't stand her! I want Elfriede to come and play!"

Frau Landmann took hold of Inge's wrists and, shaking them a little, pulled the girl to her. Standing wedged between her grandmother's knees, Inge hung her head.

"You must understand, Inge, that there are certain people whom we do not frequent. Your Elfriede is one of them. I am sure that your parents would agree with me."

Inge wished passionately that her parents were here now. She was sure that they would allow her to see her new friend. She could see no reason why they would not.

SPRING INTO WINTER

"What's wrong with Elfriede, anyway?" she wanted to know. "I wish my mother were here!"

"Now don't be unreasonable, Inge. You know that's out of the question at this time. As for what's wrong with your...friend, well, there *may* be nothing exactly wrong with her, but she comes from a very small home. A poor background. I do not know her family. She probably has bad manners."

Inge blushed, recalling Elfriede's behavior in the dairy.

"She could have an undesirable influence on you," Frau Landmann continued. "I do not wish it!" She paused dramatically, then added, "She may even have... beasts!"

"Beasts?"

"Yes. Beasts. In her hair."

Inge tittered. She imagined Elfriede's hair heaving and bulging, to part on the pointed snout of a mouse, its beady black eyes looking out at her.

"It's not a laughing matter," Frau Landmann said sternly. "These things are catching!"

Inge shook herself free impatiently. "Oh all right," she said. She was not convinced, quite the contrary. She would humor her grandmother, and proceed according to her own wishes.

The idea of 'beasts' rather attracted Inge, as did the thought of any living creature. She had never been allowed to keep pets, not even the litter of mice she had found once. Somehow, Inge was sure that the beasts to which her grandmother referred, were mice, though she could not imagine how they would live in a person's hair.

Chapter 4

If they were 'catching,' she wouldn't mind catching a few herself. She resolved to see Elfriede again at the earliest possible opportunity.

As she stored her purchases in the larder, Inge recalled the one thing she would never be able to forgive Grete. It had happened about six months earlier. Inge had been rummaging in the drawers of an old chest in the storage cellar, when she happened on a nest of chewed-up paper. In it wriggled a litter of pink, naked, newborn mice. They were blind, and so frail that she could see their organs pulsating within them. Inge's heart expanded with a gush of protective love. She took some cotton from the medicine chest in the bathroom, to make the babies more comfortable. Several times a day after that, she paid them a visit, and observed their progress. She never saw the mother mouse, but they were obviously well cared-for, because they were growing fast. When the little mice were covered in a thin sheen of silvery fur, Inge picked up the whole litter and cradled it in the hollow of one hand. They wriggled, and woffled their pink noses in the air curiously, tiny silky whiskers straining forward. At that precise moment, Grete entered the cellar to fetch a jar of preserves.

Inge held out the mice to her, wanting to share her pleasure.

But Grete shrieked, "Get these things out of here! Out of here!" She grabbed Inge by the collar and marched her, practically carried her, out to the garden. There she shook her arm so violently that the little animals fell to the ground. Then, to Inge's horror, Grete stamped on them with her heel, mashing them to a red wet pulp on the garden path.

Inge ran away and hid, sobbing wildly. She could not bear to think of the mother mouse returning home to find her babies gone. If Inge had not found them, Grete would not have seen them, either, and they would still be alive. She was eaten up with guilt, and hatred.

But that was a long time ago. I bet there are mice in Elfriede's house, Inge thought, even if there aren't any in her hair. Now that Grete is gone, I might even get some new ones, and keep them.

- Chapter 5 -

Hannelore Levy, a few months Inge's junior, was tall for her age and painfully thin. Her short dark hair curled around a bulging forehead that shadowed deep-set brown eyes; her white lips were compressed in an excess of good breeding. Frau Grünberg, an old friend of Frau Landmann's, had brought her granddaughter for afternoon coffee and cake the next day, despite Inge's pleading. Frau Grünberg's daughter had married a dentist and Hannelore was their only child.

She sat with her ankles neatly crossed and her bony hands folded in her lap. Her presence drove Inge into a frenzy of rebellion. Hannelore had often been held up to her as a model of what a *good* little girl should be. Inge detested her. She was determined this time to show the world what a sissy the girl really was, and so, make another meeting unlikely. If she was not to be allowed to have Elfriede for a friend, Inge would rather spend her days alone, than with someone like Hannelore.

Inge had carried the tray with coffee and cake to the drawing room. While waiting for the girls to leave, the two old friends were making polite conversation. Frau Landmann was tall, buxom, and majestically straight; Frau Grünberg on the other hand, was short, plump, and round-shouldered. Seen from above, her silvery head would look like a fat pin stuck in a cushion. She wore her hair parted in the middle and drawn back tightly into a hard little knot. Her nose was a button, where Frau Landmann's sallied forth with conviction. Inge's grandmother always dressed in black or dark gray, with touches of white; Frau Grünberg favored pink and pale purple. Frau Landmann smoked cigarettes, sometimes in a long ebony holder; Frau Grünberg ate chocolates, with abandon. Their friendship was a comfortable old habit.

"Come on," Inge told Hannelore, "I'll show you the doll I got for my birthday."

Hannelore looked to her grandmother for permission; Frau Grünberg nodded consent. The two girls left the room.

Hannelore was wearing a white pleated skirt with a navy blue blouse and sailor collar, and white knee socks in black patent leather strap shoes. Inge, in a washed-out blue cotton dress too short for her, was thinking up ways to mar her visitor's perfection.

As Hannelore duly admired the doll Amalia, Inge said casually, "Can you pee like a boy? Because *I* can!"

The other girl blushed and raised her eyebrows. She remained silent.

"Don't you believe me?" Inge asked. Hannelore shook her head, her lips pinched.

"All right, I'll show you. Come on!"

She led the way out the back door to the garden. On the boundary between Oma's property and the neighbor's stood a stucco garden hut with a brick-red roof. The open front faced the house, and halfway up, the other three walls were pierced by glassless windows, wooden benches running under them. Since it was surrounded by trees, the inside of the hut was in semi-darkness. The lawn and

Chapter 5

garden between it and the house had been laid on the slope of the hill, and there was a drop of about ten feet from the rear window to the neighbor's compost heap. The air smelled of old apples and sacking.

Inge climbed onto the windowsill.

"Now watch," she said, "then you try!"

She straddled her legs, pushed out her pelvis, and leaned back as far as she could without losing her balance. Then she drew back her panty bindings and lo! a stream of urine curved gracefully, splashing onto the compost below.

"See? It's easy!" Inge said as she jumped back into the hut.

Two red spots had appeared in Hannelore's pale cheeks. She put a finger in her mouth.

"Go on! You scared?"

"I... I... Oh, all right."

Desperate but defiant, Hannelore climbed onto the bench, then the window sill. Her movements were uncertain, and Inge held out a hand for support. But Hannelore ignored her. She was swaying back and forth slightly, her face ghastly with vertigo.

"It's only a few feet," Inge comforted her, "and even if you did fall, you wouldn't get hurt. The compost is soft!"

"I'm not afraid of falling," Hannelore hissed through tight lips, without moving her head.

"Go on then! What are you waiting for?"

"I don't want you to look."

"All right. I won't." Inge turned her back. Presently, she heard the liquid splashing onto the compost. She turned around.

SPRING INTO WINTER

"You see! It's easy, isn't it?"

Hannelore stood there with tears rolling down her pale cheeks.

"What's the matter?" Inge asked.

"Oooh! My good socks! They're ruined!"

Inge was convulsed with laughter. She bent double, clasping her stomach, and hooted with delight. "Oh, oh, oh!" she gasped, "it's too funny! It's killing me! What's your Oma going to say, that you wetted yourself?"

Hannelore jumped down. "You beast! I hate you! You did this on purpose!"

"What do you mean? I did it too, didn't I? Oh-oh, wetting yourself, at your age!" She doubled over in a new access of mirth. "You know," she added, "you're not so bad, after all. At least you've got guts. Come on, I'll show you a secret."

She grabbed Hannelore by the hand and pulled her along. At first, the other girl resisted, then, as before a strong wind, she gave in. "I know where Oma keeps my grandfather's cigars," Inge said. "We'll go and take a couple."

"That's stealing!"

"Puh! Nobody smokes them now, anyway."

"Have you? Smoked one, I mean?"

"Uh-hunh. They're good. My grandfather smoked only the best, of course. Havanas."

Inge did not mention that the first time she had smoked one, she had been horribly sick.

Hannelore was impressed. She went along silently for a while.

"Havana," she said. "That's in Cuba."

Chapter 5

"I don't know. Why?"

"Well, as a matter of fact, we're going there, next December. To Cuba. I'm not supposed to talk about it."

"You can tell me! I'm good at keeping secrets. As a matter of fact..."

"What?"

Inge shrugged. "Oh, nothing. It's a secret, and I'm not telling."

"If you won't tell me yours, I won't tell you mine."

Inge skipped a few steps. "Stupid!" she said, "you already have!"

Hannelore compressed her lips. Inge noticed that she was walking with her legs slightly spread, like a sailor who had not yet regained his land legs.

"What's the matter? You uncomfortable?" she asked.

Hannelore nodded, blushing.

"Come on up to my room. I'll lend you a pair of socks. And pants too, if you need them."

In her room, Inge whistled softly under her breath while she gazed out of the window. The street meandered quietly up into the woods. The only sign of life was a woman walking her dog. Hannelore changed her clothes in silence.

"Why didn't your mother come today?" Inge asked.

"She's working. She has to help my father in the office. Someone has to. He can't have Aryans any more."

"I forgot....Then who does the cooking in your house?"

"My grandmother. She makes beans all the time. Green beans. I don't like them."

"My Oma does the cooking now, too. Since Grete left. She's a great cook, roast chicken nearly every day. I love

53

chicken." She glanced at Hannelore, to see if she believed this. "Chicken is very expensive," she added.

"So what," Hannelore said. "I had oysters once."

Inge grinned and gave her a friendly shove. "I was only kidding," she said. Noticing that Hannelore was holding her soiled clothes uncertainly, she said, "Just dump them in the washbasin. You can pick them up later. And wait here, I'll be right back."

Inge went into Frau Landmann's bedroom and opened the walk-in closet, where the box of cigars was stored in the drawer of a folding desk. The tobacco, and the cedar wood of the cigar box, perfumed the entire closet. Inge loved the straw-dry rasping scent. It was so strong and firm, so different from the subtle odors of her world dominated by women. She took two of the black cigars, and picked up the box of matches from her grandmother's bedside table.

The two girls climbed the stairs to the laundry room.

"In case of fire," Inge explained, "so we're near water." She noted with glee Hannelore's involuntary shudder.

Inge climbed into the washtub and motioned to Hannelore to join her. They sat cross-legged; the rough stone felt cold on the skin of their thighs. Their heads came only just above the rim of the tub. Inge bit off the closed end of her cigar and spit it onto the floor.

"Opa used to do this with a neat little silver gadget, but I couldn't find it," she said. "Go on, you bite some off too, or it won't draw."

Hannelore turned the cigar over and over in her fingers. Finally, she bit off a piece, and gagged.

Chapter 5

"It tastes better when you smoke it," Inge assured her. "Just wait."

She stuck the cigar in her mouth, struck a match under it, and drew in the smoke. Screwing up her eyes, she puffed rapidly. Then she handed the box of matches to Hannelore and sat back, watching her.

Hannelore's hands were shaking so that she had to strike three matches before she succeeded in lighting her cigar. She inhaled, and choked violently. Tears ran down her cheeks. But she tried again. And again. Her face turned green. The cigar slipped from her fingers. She clapped a hand over her mouth, leaned over the side of the tub, and threw up on the floor.

Inge jumped up and stamped on the cigar to extinguish it. She crossed her arms on her chest. "Well," she said, "I think that's enough for today. Let's clean up this mess."

They climbed out of the tub, Hannelore on wobbly legs. As she surveyed the sorry picture her victim made, Inge felt a twinge of remorse. "Here," she said, "you go and sit down over there. I'll mop up."

"I want to go home!" Hannelore wailed after a while. "You are mean, and I hate you!"

Inge shrugged. "I can't help it if you have a weak stomach," she said self-righteously. "I hope you'll be happy in Havana! That's where they make cigars. *Every*body there smokes them!"

"Oh-oh-oh! I want my mother! I want to go home!"

"Come on, cry-baby. I'll take you to your Oma."

SPRING INTO WINTER

As she was seeing the visitors off at the front door, Frau Landmann looked suspiciously at Inge out of the corner of her eyes. "I'd like to have a little chat with you, young lady," she said, turning back into the house.

In the drawing room, Frau Landmann threw open the double windows, gathered up the cushions from the deep armchair where her guest had been sitting, punched them vigorously, and flung them to air on the windowsills.

"I'll bet that woman hasn't taken a bath since her husband-God-rest-his-soul passed on, five years ago!"

"I thought Frau Grünberg was your friend!" Inge challenged.

"So she is, child, so she is." Frau Landmann turned to Inge and added, "But that doesn't stop her from smelling!"

The old lady sat down heavily in her own chair and patted her knee. "Come sit here with me," she said.

Inge shuffled around the carved table, dragging her feet.

"Lift your feet!" Frau Landmann said.

Inge sat stiffly on her grandmother's lap and stared down at her dangling feet.

"Well?" the old lady said, "out with it!"

"Out with what?"

"What did you do to your friend to make her sick?"

"She isn't my friend."

"That's not the point. You were unkind to a guest. I want to know what you have done."

"Oh...nothing. She just has a weak stomach I guess. The cake didn't agree with her." Inge looked sideways at Frau Landmann.

Chapter 5

"Stop fooling!" So she didn't believe her. "Let me smell your breath! Have you been to the wine cellar?"

"Of course not!" Inge was indignant. "I wouldn't do that! Besides, *you* have the key."

"Blow!" the old lady commanded.

Reluctantly, Inge complied.

Frau Landmann sniffed, then leaned back. "Aha!" she said. "Tobacco!"

Inge studied her fingernails, swinging her legs. She nearly slid off her grandmother's lap. Oma grabbed her arm.

"Where did you get it?" she asked.

"In your bedroom," Inge mumbled.

"Opa's cigars? You mean to say you... and that poor child...smoked...?"

Inge nodded. She was miserable with guilt. Frau Landmann was silent. Then, gently at first and from deep within her, she started to shake, then to heave, then to rock, as she gave in to laughter. She crowed and hooted and roared, tears of hilarity running down her papery cheeks.

"You horrible child, you!" she gasped, "you'll be the death of me!"

Inge's lips twitched, turned down at the corners. Suddenly remorseful, her eyes filled with tears. But then, she was infected by her grandmother's laughter. Her high clear voice joined Frau Landmann's booming one, and they hugged each other, aching with mirth. Oma produced a handkerchief, dried her eyes, and blew her nose with a sound like a trumpet blast.

"You know," she said, and she had to bite her lips to prevent another explosion, "that was very, very unkind of you. And naughty. The poor girl!" She took a shuddering breath and again wiped her eyes. "By the way," she said, "how come *you* didn't get sick?"

"Oh, I'm used to it."

"What! Do you mean to say...?"

"Uh-huh," Inge nodded. "I've done it before."

"And?"

"Well, I got sick the first time. Then I found that if I blew out the smoke straight away, I wouldn't get sick. So that's how I did it. Simple."

"Only you forgot to give that bit of advice to your... to Hannelore, eh?"

Inge rubbed her palms together and blushed. Frau Landmann went on, "What grudge do you have against the poor child? She's never done you any harm!"

"She's so damn good, she makes me sick, is all!"

"Don't swear," old lady said automatically. Then she sighed. "Oh, well. I can see your point....But," and her voice became stern, "don't ever do such a thing again! A host has a duty to treat his guests kindly, and be helpful. And don't you forget it." She ruffled Inge's smooth hair. "Oh, before I forget..." she added, "the new girl is arriving in two days. I am counting on you to do your best to make her feel welcome. Is that clear? And now, run away. I want to rest."

- Chapter 6 -

Frau Landmann was using her cane to dig out weeds around a rose bush by the front door, when the squeak of the garden gate made her look up. Doris Kahn had arrived, carrying a yellow pigskin suitcase in a manicured hand. It was the fifteenth of August.

"Oh my heavens! What have we here?" Frau Landmann muttered under her breath as she watched the young girl mince up the garden path on very high heels. However, she boomed heartily, "Welcome, young lady! I hope you'll be happy with us!" and shook the young girl's hand vigorously.

Doris Kahn winced. At nineteen, she was a short, plump girl. Her blue eyes were fringed with black lashes, although her massive mop of crinkly hair was ginger. She had the bluish freckled skin often seen on redheads. Her nose was delicately arched.

Doris had been studying nursing, but was forced to stop because of the numeric restrictions imposed on Jews admitted to teaching institutions. Not enough Jewish hospitals were available to absorb all the evicted student nurses. Doris's father had been interned in a concentration camp for six months, then released, a man destroyed. He tried, without success, to pick up what was left of a once-prosperous business. His daughter now had to earn a living, and she resented the necessity.

SPRING INTO WINTER

Frau Landmann made valiant efforts to suppress her innate haughtiness, and did her best to make Doris feel like a member of the family, without however forgetting the purpose of her presence. Doris ate at table with her and Inge, whereas Grete had always taken her meals in the kitchen. Under the old lady's supervision, Doris learned to cook and clean. She made the beds and, much to Inge's relief, took over the shopping in the village.

Little by little, Doris settled into her new situation, and her eyes were not so often red-rimmed at breakfast time. Sometimes, in a sweet throaty voice, she sang Zionist songs, that Inge had never heard. Doris's dream was to go to Palestine and work on a cooperative farm, a kibbutz.

"Well, young lady," Frau Landmann commented the day she was told about this, "now is your chance to get into the habit of hard work!" She winked before Doris could take offense at the remark.

Doris took over the room vacated by Grete. Her stiff attempts at friendliness struck Inge as condescension. There was a distance between them that had never existed between her and Grete, who had known her since infancy. Perhaps a closer bond, a comradeship could have developed between the two girls, since Doris was only nine years older than Inge. But the awkwardness never left Doris entirely. It was as though she had cloaked herself in resentment, and it was obvious that she thought herself too good for the menial tasks she was asked to perform. But eventually, Inge's curiosity and good nature wore her down.

Chapter 6

At first, Doris tried to keep her fingernails immaculately painted, but she soon found that washing dishes and scrubbing floors chipped the nail polish, and that looked worse than none at all. Her high-heeled shoes also were quickly discarded in favor of low-heeled ones.

One day, Inge asked her idly if she had her fingernails painted when she was nursing, too. Doris was huffed.

"Of course not!" she said. "I only did them on my days off."

"Do you have a boy friend?"

"Mind your own business!"

"I only asked! No need to get stuffy!" Inge twirled on her heel. "Grete got married when she left here," she said.

"So what. Was it anyone you knew?"

"Yes. The coalman. He hates Jews and cheated Oma with the coal."

"Why did Grete marry him, then?"

"She had to marry *some*one. She had nowhere to go. Besides, she wasn't Jewish. So what could the poor woman do?"

"Anyway," Doris said, "I'll thank you not to compare me to your grandmother's maid. I'm not a servant. I'm only helping out temporarily. Because I want to."

Inge shrugged. She thought Doris silly, because she herself loved Grete and valued her greatly. She saw nothing wrong with being Oma's maid. Once girls reached the age of her sister Erika, they became a mystery: all mixed up and haughty, up one moment and down the next.

But her curiosity was not satisfied.

"Doris?" she went on.

"What is it?"

"If a German boy asked you, I mean an Aryan, would you let him kiss you?"

"Of course not! Kiss me? Who told you about kissing? Of course I wouldn't let him!"

"Of course not! Of course not! That's all you say. Why not? What's wrong with it, anyway? Were you kosher at your house?"

Doris had to laugh. "I don't see what being kosher has to do with it," she said. "After all, boys aren't for eating!"

Inge, not to be sidetracked, went on, "Well, were you? Kosher, I mean?"

"As a matter of fact, my family does keep a kosher kitchen."

"So how do you manage with us? Since we don't."

"Oh, that's all right. I myself am not that strict."

"Does your mother wear a wig?" Inge asked. She knew that Orthodox Jewish women wore wigs after marriage.

"No. We aren't that orthodox."

"So why wouldn't you have an Aryan boyfriend?"

"Don't you ever stop asking questions? First of all, it's forbidden by law."

"Oh, *their* law...!" Inge was scornful.

"Ours, too. And I want to go to Palestine and marry someone there."

"You got someone you know?"

Chapter 6

Doris blushed. "It's none of your business. I told you before....As a matter of fact, I do have someone over there. And he's waiting for me."

"Well! Who would have thought it?" Inge performed an Indian war dance around Doris, chanting, "Doris has a boyfriend! Doris has a boyfriend!"

The older girl made a grab for Inge, but missed. Inge skipped away laughing, and poked out her tongue.

"You get out of here, you horrid child!" Doris gasped, furious and near tears. She tried another swipe, and missed again. "If I had known you were part of your grandmother's household, I wouldn't have come, you may be sure of that!"

The four weeks' summer vacation came to an end. Inge had entered the Lyzeum, the girls' high school, at Easter, when the new school year had started. She had joined a year earlier than she would have under normal circumstances, because the elementary school she had attended in Cologne, her hometown, had a more intensive curriculum than the local Barmen one; thus, she had been able to skip one class. Both her mother and her aunt had attended the Lyzeum in their youth. At that time, it had been called the "High School for Higher Daughters." Now, as then, it was attended mainly by the daughters of the more well-to-do citizens, with a sprinkling of scholarship students, to pander to democracy. By now, Inge was the only Jewish child left, among the hundred and fifty or so pupils.

"Heil Hitler!" Herr Bauer, the class teacher, called out crisply, standing behind his raised desk. His arm was raised in the Nazi salute.

It was the first school day after the vacation. Shoes scraping on the wooden floor with a hollow sound, the girls rose at the teacher's entrance.

"Heil Hitler!" they replied in unison, every right arm lifted at the correct angle. All but Inge's.

"You may sit." Herr Bauer sat on the chair behind his desk and added, "Welcome back to school. I hope that you will work hard, as good German girls should. Time for play is over. Now, roll call!"

"Amhorst, Elsbeth!" Herr Bauer started.

"Present." A thin blonde girl stood up. The teacher looked up, made a note on his list, and went on.

"Apfel, Annemarie."

"Present."

"Brenner, Holga."

"Present."

"Erlenmayer, Kristine."

"Present."

He read down the list of twenty names. Inge's was the last.

"Ahhh!" As he reached it, Herr Bauer took a deep breath. He leaned back and crossed his arms, tapping a foot on the floor. A smile twitched his thin lips. In the expectant silence, a heat-drowsy fly bumped against a window pane before bumbling into freedom through the opening. "Ah, our Jew, Richter, Sarah. Richter, stand up!"

Inge stood up awkwardly, her face flaming red. Her fair hair appeared even fairer in contrast. What was this 'Sarah'?

Chapter 6

"Girls, take a good look at this Jew. You won't have many more chances to see one."

There was scattered tittering in the class. Irmgard Lumpe, a pale dark-haired girl at the desk next to Inge's, reached out and gently touched her hand. Irmgard had asked Inge to her home once, before the vacation. She lived with her sister, mother, and father in a small apartment on the other side of town; because her father was a veteran blinded in the 1914-1918 war, Irmgard attended the Lyzeum on a scholarship.

"Lumpe!" the teacher roared, "move back two rows!"

Irmgard complied in silence, her lips white. The other girls shifted, to make room for her. A void was left around Inge.

"Please, sir," she said, "my name is..."

"Shut your mouth! Who gave you permission to speak?"

Herr Bauer was a small man. His complexion was sallow and he often had a pimple reddening the skin beside his sharp nose. His brown hair was sleeked back from a high narrow forehead. He limped, and used a cane. It was his pride that he bore a slight resemblance to Dr. Goebbels, the Minister for Propaganda.

Herr Bauer taught history. German History. Now he unhooked his cane from the back of his chair and laid it across the desk, tapping the wooden surface lightly.

"So," he said softly, "you object to the name Sarah?"

Inge nodded, swallowed. "My name is..."

"Sarah!" Herr Bauer finished for her. "Sarah. Don't you know that Jews will no longer carry Aryan names?"

Inge shook her head. The girls snickered.

SPRING INTO WINTER

"Silence!" the teacher roared. "Let me explain to the Jew child!" Again he crossed his arms. The fingers of his right hand played scales on his left arm. "As of last week, August 20th, to be precise," he continued in a silky voice, female Jews are to put the good Jewish name of Sarah before their given one. Israel, if they happen to be male. So there won't be any mistake. A name like Ingeborg, a good German name, is defiled," he pushed his face forward and, his voice leaping into a higher register, screamed, "*defiled* by a Jew! Now, Richter, Sarah, are you satisfied?"

Bubbles of spit had appeared at the corners of Herr Bauer's mouth. Inge sat down and did not reply.

"Up! Up, Jew!"

Inge jumped up.

"Who gave you permission to sit? You will stand during the lesson, so we can all have a good look at you. We wouldn't want to forget you, would we, girls?"

The history lesson proceeded. Inge was studiously ignored. Once in a while, Herr Bauer clip-clopped down the aisle between the pupils, circled Inge, and thwacked his stick on her desk. Each time, Inge jumped a little.

Her legs were beginning to ache. She stood immobile in her place, swaying slightly, her arms straight beside her. Only her fists were clenched, the nails digging little crescents into her palms.

At last the bell rang. The girls sprang to attention, shouting the Nazi salute. Inge's right arm also rose automatically; it seemed like a reflex, for self-preservation. Herr Bauer limped over to her furiously, and with his stick slammed down her arm. Tears stung her eyes at

Chapter 6

the pain.

"Our Führer does not need your salute! I forbid you to defile his name!" Herr Bauer spat. He hobbled to the door and swung it open. "Heil Hitler!' he barked.

"Heil Hitler!" the chorus of girls' voices sang again, all except Inge's.

When Herr Bauer had left the room, Inge sat white-faced at her desk, rubbing her arm where a red welt had developed, and stared into space. Only during the next lesson, English, did she come to life again.

Fräulein Gerhardus, the teacher, was a mild-mannered, gentle spinster in her forties. Her face was pock-marked from a childhood disease. Pupils and teachers alike despised her as too soft for her own good, and tended to take advantage of her.

Fräulein Gerhardus did not mention the new law about names, and Inge was deeply grateful.

During English, Irmgard Lumpe had moved back to her desk next to Inge's. Now, as the bell rang for recess and the girls started to file out to the schoolyard, Christel, a tall flaxen-haired girl hissed at Irmgard, "Jew lover! I'll tell Herr Bauer that you've moved back!"

"Go away, do, and leave us alone," Irmgard said coldly. She turned her back on the other girl and took Inge's hand. "Come on, we'll play together."

As they stood talking in a corner of the yard, a group of bigger girls came up and surrounded them. One of them yanked Irmgard away.

"What do you think you are doing?" she said. "Do you want to be taken for a Jew? Don't you have any pride?"

SPRING INTO WINTER

Irmgard was not used to having her behavior criticized. Her home life, based on mutual understanding and respect, had early taught her to make her own decisions. She shook off the girl's hand. Her brown eyes blazed. "I didn't ask for your opinion," she said. "I'll talk and play with whom I please!"

"If that's the way you want it....I hope you know what you are doing. You'll have only yourself to blame for the consequences." The tall girl swung away, took the arms of two of her friends and led the whole group over to the opposite side of the yard.

Meanwhile a knot of Inge's classmates had formed not far off.

"Christ killer! Christ killer!" they now started chanting. Inge began to shake.

"Don't take any notice of them," Irmgard told her and took her by the shoulders to turn her away from the girls. "Just pretend they're not here."

Presently a fat little girl with red pigtails detached herself from the others, came up behind the two, and kicked Inge in the hollow of her knees. Inge's legs buckled, but she made a quick recovery and whirled around, flaming with rage. The other child spat squarely in her face.

"Dirty Jew! You killed Jesus!" she shrieked.

Inge wiped the spit from her face with her sleeve. Her lips worked silently, then she said clearly, "Your Jesus was a Jew himself!"

A gasp of horror escaped from the bunch of girls.

"Did you hear that? Did you hear what she said? Let's go tell Herr Doktor!"

Chapter 6

They moved away, their arms around each other, whispering fiercely. They looked back at Inge over their shoulders, their clean little-girl faces distorted with hatred.

Herr Doktor Gretz, the Director of the school, was a tall man, and his light reddish hair was beginning to turn white. He sat behind his desk, his knotty hands folded on the green blotter in front of him. Looking at Inge through horn-rimmed spectacles, he said, "Sit down, child. There's no need to be afraid."

Inge perched on the edge of a chair facing the Director. Her feet dangled; they did not reach the ground.

When Inge's mother and aunt had attended the school, Herr Doktor Gretz had been simply Herr Gretz, and teaching mathematics. The school was his whole life. He now sighed deeply, and passed a hand over his face.

"Times have changed since I taught your mother, Ingeborg," he said. "And I wish they had not."

Inge rolled the hem of her dress tightly in her fingers. Her knuckles showed white. She waited.

"Your classmates tell me," the principal went on, "that you said Jesus was a Jew."

Inge lifted her chin. "He was, too!" she said. "You *know* he was!"

A smile appeared and vanished on the Doktor's face.

"You know and I know that he was," he admitted. "And so do a lot of other people. But," he cleared his throat and appeared embarrassed, "we have orders not to mention that fact in our schools. German children are not supposed to...to know...that...Christ was...a...Jew." He emphasized every word, as though to punish himself for his obedience to mindless power. "So there it is."

He pushed his palms against the edge of the desk and lifted his shoulders in a defeated shrug.

"*You* know you are right. The other girls don't know any better, and they think they are right. Be a clever girl, Inge, don't fight them. For your own preservation." Again the Director sighed. "I wish I could help you," he said. "But the school comes before all else, and for the good of the school, I have to follow orders." He stood up and crossed over to Inge. Placing a hand on her shoulder he said: "It would be best, perhaps, if your grandmother withdrew you now."

Inge looked up at him, stricken. "From the school?" she asked. "You want me to leave the school?"

"Don't you want to leave?" Inge shook her head vehemently, her hair whipping around her face. "Not even after the way they treated you today?" the Director asked.

Again Inge shook her head. She stuck out her chin.

"Especially not now!" she said.

Doktor Gretz sighed. "You do have spirit, girl, I'll give you that. May it help you... may it help you."

He took a few steps across the office and back, chin in hand. "Well," he said at last, "let's wait a while and see how things work out. You are the only Jewish girl left in the school, you know that, don't you?" Inge nodded. "And you don't *look* Jewish," Herr Doktor Gretz went on. "No, indeed, you don't. If the other students had not known it already, they would not have been any the wiser." He passed a finger gently down Inge's forehead,

Chapter 6

nose and chin, tracing her profile. "How like your mother you look," he said, shaking his head.

Inge blushed. She felt that the Director had meant the statement as a compliment, and did not know how to react. It was a good thing right now, wasn't it, not to look Jewish? But should she feel pleased at the Director's opinion? She did feel pleased, and was ashamed of it.

- Chapter 7 -

Inge said nothing at home of the events at school that first day. She was afraid that if her grandmother knew, she would want to withdraw her. Preoccupied with her own thoughts, Frau Landmann appeared satisfied with the noncommittal answer to her question, "How was school?"

With the exception of Irmgard Lumpe, everyone at school left Inge alone the next day and the following ones. It was as though teachers and pupils had tacitly agreed to ignore the Jewish girl in their midst. Inge felt abandoned, yet grateful for the relative peace, and she was buoyed by Irmgard's friendly proximity.

A few days later, at breakfast which Frau Landmann, Doris and Inge now took in the conservatory, there was a photo-postcard for Inge. It had come from Belgium, and pictured her father standing beside a medium-sized French car, a Citroën, parked at the curb. He was squinting at the camera, his spectacles glinting in the sun. He looked a lot thinner than Inge remembered him. But it was more than two years since she had last seen him, and perhaps her memory was unsure. On the back of the card her father had scrawled: "Don't forget your Prickly Bear!"

Nothing else. He had not signed the card. Inge swallowed hard. "Prickly Bear" had been Inge'sprivate name for her father. He used to rub his unshaven chin against

Chapter 7

Inge's cheek in the morning, before breakfast. On the photograph, he had half-extended a hand towards the car, and the photographer had caught him at that moment when he seemed to think better of pretending that the car was his. A sad little smile pulled down the corners of his mouth. Up to the time of his hurried flight from Germany in 1936, Herr Richter had owned a Mercedes-Benz. Chauffeur-driven. Silently, Inge handed the photo to her grandmother.

Frau Landmann was reading a letter that also bore a Belgian stamp. She took the card from Inge without lifting her eyes from the letter, nodded her thanks, and laid it beside her plate. Doris poured more coffee into the cup that the old lady held out to her.

"Thank you, girl," she said, and slurped noisily. Turning to Inge, she added, "This is a letter from your mother. Listen to what she has to say..." She scanned the loosely written pages, searching for the passage. "Ah, here we are. Now listen. 'I have made arrangements for Erika's departure directly from Berlin." Frau Landmann interrupted herself, her face indignant. "That means," she accused, "that your sister won't be allowed to come and say good-bye! It's a scandal. A scandal, I say!"

The old lady fumbled for her handkerchief and blew her nose. "And this is how she goes on, your precious mother. Listen. 'I have instructed her carefully in the steps to take. There are people who will help her across the border, and I shall meet her in Malmédy on the 12th, God willing. We shall start a little household again, at last, and soon you and our little Inge will join us here.' Ha, we'll see about *that*! 'So, dearest Mother,'" here the old lady again blew her nose, "unfortunately you won't be able to see Erika before she leaves.' Didn't I say so? A scandal! 'Hans and I think it is best so,'--I bet your father was behind this!--'since this way, she can still help Lydia and her family get ready for their departure on the 15th.'"

Erika had spent this last year in Berlin with their aunt Lydia, Frau Landmann's younger daughter. Inge gaped in amazement. She had had no idea that Erika was due to leave Germany. And so soon! Only one more week....Nor had she known of her aunt's intended departure. Oma had not told her.

"When will *we* be going, Oma?" she asked.

"It'll be a while yet. I have to wind up things here first, and then I suppose your mother will come and pick you up. She has already applied for your visa."

Inge had heard the word "visa" so often that she was familiar with it, without however understanding its meaning. She knew only that it was one of the official documents necessary to "get out". And that it was difficult to obtain.

"Has Erika got a visa, then?"

Frau Landmann shook her head. "No," she said. "She could not get a passport."

"Why not? How is she going to get out, then?"

"Why not, why not! *I* don't know why not. Why do they do any of these things? God only knows....I hope they'll come to their senses soon. But there are other ways of getting out....There *are* ways."

The old lady's eyes became vague. Her hand was lying on the postcard that Inge had given her. Presently,

Chapter 7

her fingers sent to her wandering mind the message of what they were touching. She looked down.

"So!" she said, "you have mail, too!" She smiled at Inge, then studied her son-in-law's appearance. "Mmmm..." she commented, "a bit down in the mouth, I'd say....Always a clown, that Hans. Does he really believe he'd fool anyone, standing by that car?"

Inge blushed, ashamed for her father.

"Maybe he bought a new car?" she suggested.

Frau Landmann raised her eyebrows and made "Ha!" She had a poor opinion of both her sons-in-law, but of Inge's father especially. She had always maintained that her daughters could have done a lot better for themselves, forgetting that she herself had nipped in the bud several promising romances with well-to-do young men, because they were Gentiles.

Before his flight into exile, Inge's father had been the owner of a printing plant. Warned by a German friend who had government connections that the confiscation of his plant was imminent, and that he would be sent to a concentration camp, Herr Richter had fled the country with nothing but the clothes he was wearing. Inge remembered getting postcards from all the countries where he had stopped for a while. There was one from Serbia she remembered in particular. It was a garishly tinted portrait of the young king of that country, and her father had written on the reverse, "Doesn't he look like a fairy-tale prince?"

The fact that Herr Richter had been successful in his work did nothing to raise his stock in Frau Landmann's eyes. He was a self-made man, and his father had been a cattle merchant. Frau Landmann insisted that her son-in-law had never quite shed the odor of goats and cows.

"A new car?" she now scoffed. "Don't make me laugh! Why, he hasn't even the means to buy a new suit--which he sorely needs, by the look of him!"

Inge was close to tears. "You aren't very nice about my father, Oma," she said. "Why don't you like him?"

"Who said I don't like him?" Frau Landmann blustered. "He's all right--I suppose. Though an honest man would not abandon his children in the lion's den!"

"That's unfair! You know it's unfair! He could not have taken us along!"

"Don't you dare talk back to me! I know what I know," Frau Landmann said cryptically. She picked up objects on the table, only to set them down elsewhere, and avoided looking at Inge, as though ashamed of her outburst.

Frau Landmann had always kept her eyes resolutely closed to her son-in-law's qualities. She refused to acknowledge his devotion to her daughter, his somewhat erratic love of his children, and the fact that he was more than a good provider.

She did not like her other son-in-law much better. He was a physician, as his father had been before him, so she could not base her dislike on her social prejudices. She resented him simply for marrying her younger daughter Lydia, who had been expected to make a brilliant career as a concert pianist. Instead, she had chosen to throw herself away in marriage and become a housewife.

Chapter 7

On the other hand, Frau Landmann had approved of her son's choice of a wife. He had brought home a meek little thing of good family, properly in awe of her mother-in-law. She had borne four children whose future Frau Landmann had already planned, when her son, without consulting her nor asking her permission, had taken his family off to Australia--to the other side of the world. Frau Landmann had been both outraged and heartbroken.

Inge was frantically searching for a question that would change the tenor of the conversation. "Oma," she managed at last, "do I have a passport? Or did they refuse to give me one, too?"

"You don't need one of your own yet." Frau Landmann gratefully fell in with the new subject. "You are too young, and your name is entered on your mother's passport. Since hers is still valid, you don't have to worry."

"And you, Oma? Do you have one?"

"Heavens, yes! It's seen a good bit of service, too...."

With her husband, Frau Landmann had traveled abroad yearly, to Italy, to Greece, and France, the Canary Islands, Palestine, Egypt. In the year of Inge's birth, Herr and Frau Landmann had even made a trip to America on the luxury liner "Bremen." Their arrival had been announced in the social columns of the New York papers, and upon their return, Frau Landmann had had the clippings framed. They now lay forgotten in a drawer of the study desk, witnesses to a glorious past.

"How is Erika going to get over there? To Belgium, I mean," Inge persisted.

"I have no idea, child. Your mother didn't tell me. Besides, the less we know, the less we are likely to give away."

Frau Landmann squinted at the gold watch pinned to her dress at the end of a chain. "Isn't it about time for school?" she asked. "Your tram is due any moment."

The old lady handed her plate to Doris, who had been coming and going, sitting down to eat when she did not have to fetch and carry. Inge and her grandmother had become so accustomed to her presence, that she in no way inhibited their little quarrels and disputes.

Inge kissed Frau Landmann good-bye, greeted Doris, picked up her school satchel in the cloakroom, and crossed the street to the tram stop. From there, she looked back at her grandmother's house. Autumn was not far away now. Soon the vine crawling up the house would be blood-red against the stucco walls.

Inge had walked up and down the hill road several times, hoping that Elfriede would see her, and ask her into her house. But so far, she had had no luck. Elfriede had remained invisible. After school on September 14, Inge finally decided that she had to take matters into her own hands. Since Elfriede did not go to the same school, Inge had no other way to find out what was the matter.

She walked boldly up to the door of the slate house; its green paint was cracked. Inge banged the tarnished brass knocker. After a while, she heard shuffling footsteps draw close, then the door creaked open.

Chapter 7

A pale woman looked at her out of lashless eyes. White-blond hair escaped in wisps from the loose knot at her nape. She was wearing a faded blue overall belted at the waist, and flaccid breasts flopped loosely under the thin cotton cloth. Trodden-down slippers clung to her bare feet. The smell of boiled cabbage and dishwater streamed past her out of the house and into the clear air.

"Is Elfriede home?" Inge asked, twisting her hands nervously.

Without answering Inge's question, the woman said, "Aren't you the Jewish kid from up the hill?"

Inge nodded, blushing.

"Well, come on in!" The woman jerked her head toward the interior of the house. "I'm Elfriede's mom. She's in there."

She led the way through a lobby paved with worn stone slabs into a living-room-kitchen at right.

Across from the door stood a black iron coal range; a kettle steamed on its rings. The room was stifling hot and sparely lit by two small windows hung with crocheted string curtains. The scrubbed plank floor was lustreless. Elfriede was sitting at a table covered with newspapers, darning a man's sock stretched over a round form. Dark blue shadows lay under her eyes. As Inge entered, she looked up and grinned. Between her pale lips, her teeth seemed even yellower.

"Hello..." Inge said awkwardly. "Are you sick?"

"Oh, I'm all right, now. I'm going back to school tomorrow. How about you?"

"I'm fine. I thought I'd come and see you..."

SPRING INTO WINTER

Inge stood beside the table, twisting her hands. Elfriede's mother, arms crossed on her chest, was watching her. At last, she pulled a chair from under the table.

"Might as well sit down, as you're here," she said.

Inge smiled quickly, said "Thank you," and sat down at the edge of the chair.

"I haven't seen you for ages," she said to Elfriede.

The girl nodded. "Yes, I know. I've been sick."

"What's the matter?"

"Oh, nothing much. I get it now and then. Cough, cough, cough. And then I spit."

"Weak chest, our Elfriede," her mother said.

"Oh." Inge wondered what to say next, but the woman's presence paralyzed her tongue.

"Ma!" a man's voice called from the back of the house, "where're my socks?"

Elfriede's mother jumped. "That's our Willi," she said, running out a door at the other end of the kitchen. Red spots had appeared in her sallow cheeks.

Elfriede motioned after her mother. "My brother," she explained. "He's grown-up." She stopped, searching for words. Then she said, "He's a storm trooper. In the S.A."

Inge shivered. A brown-shirt, here in the house! The S.A., the famous *Sturm Abteilung*, was a nationally organized band of uniformed Hitler supporters known for their hatred of Jews, their militant anti-Semitism. Inge stood up hurriedly and went toward the door.

"I'd better be going," she said. "I only came to ask you over, for tomorrow. My grandmother's going to be away."

Chapter 7

Elfriede smiled a little, her hands idle in front of her. "You needn't be afraid of our Willi," she said. "He can't do anything to you. Our Dad's a policeman, and *he*'d tell him what!"

Inge glanced nervously at the door through which Elfriede's mother had left. She scraped the tip of her shoe on the floor. "I'm not afraid," she lied. "Will you come over tomorrow? After school?"

"Yes, all right. But don't go yet!"

"I must get back, or Oma will wonder where I am." She reached the door to the lobby and turned around. "By the way," she said, "I don't even know your last name!"

"Flasche," Elfriede said. "What's yours? I know your Oma's, Landmann. Everybody knows *her*."

"Mine's Richter."

The other door burst open and a tow-haired young man in a storm-trooper's black riding pants and brown shirt strode into the room. He was carrying his shiny black boots and gaiters in his hand.

"Richter!" he sneered, "that's not a Jew name!"

Inge shrank back against the door, groping behind her for the handle. She swallowed, and said nothing.

"Hey, Ma," the young man went on as his mother appeared behind him, "what d'you think you're doing, having a Jew brat in the house?"

"Leave the kid be," Frau Flasche said, "I told you she's visiting with our Elfriede."

"She's a Jew and she has no business here."

"You should be ashamed, picking on a child!'

"A Jew child's as bad as an old Jew." He waved a stubby finger at Inge. "You get out of here, you!'

SPRING INTO WINTER

"Shut your mouth or I'll tell your Pa on you!" Frau Flasche lifted a hand as though to strike her son.

"Don't you dare touch me!" Willi's small blue eyes narrowed. He stuck his chin out close his mother's face and snarled, "I'm a good German, I am, and I won't have Jews in my house!"

Frau Flasche gave her son a shove and put her hands on her hips. "As long's your Pa's paying the rent, it isn't your house, and don't you forget it. And stop trying to bully me. I'm still your Ma!"

"Ma or no Ma," Willi said, a little uncertainly now, "I'll report you if you...if you fraternize with the Enemy!"

"Oh, get away with you!" His mother shrugged. "The Enemy! Don't make me laugh. Look at her! The Enemy!"

Inge wished she could have been invisible during this exchange. She groped for the door handle behind her, and turning around found it higher than she had thought. Opening the door, she fled to the entrance. Behind her, she heard Elfriede call, "See you tomorrow, Inge!"

Then Willi's voice, threatening, "Sarah! Sarah! Don't you dare show your crooked nose in this place again, Sarah!"

"Shut up!" Frau Flasche's angry yell was the last thing Inge heard as she ran down the worn stone steps to the street.

Her heart was beating high in her throat, and she was shaking. And with all this, she thought, I've even forgotten to ask about mice. The house must be hundreds of years old, there are sure to be mice.

Chapter 7

Inge was calming down little by little, but to gain some more time, she decided to go home the long way, cutting through a corner of the woods. Near the entrance at the top of Frau Landmann's street, where the woods ended, there was an open-air café, the *Waldhaus*. Sometimes on a Sunday, Inge and her grandmother would go there for hot chocolate and a pretzel, or a sugar cone filled with whipped cream. A couple of monkeys lived there in a spacious cage, and peacocks strutted about freely, calling their raucous "Lee-on! Lee-on!" Inge collected the eyed feathers that fell out of the males' tails. Soon, the Waldhaus would be closed for winter, and there would not be another chance to get feathers before next year. Now might be a good time to get some. The owners had always been friendly, filling Inge's sugar cones with cream right down to the very tip.

Leaves, translucent gold with approaching autumn, floated down one by one from the birches. The earth was rich with the scent of fungi, and red squirrels were gathering their winter store of acorns. Down to the right, invisible behind beech and sycamore, was a meadow sliced by a little brook. The tall grass was patchy with sorrel and clover. Frogs croaked into the still, scented afternoon.

In spring, the sodden spongy soil squelching underfoot, Inge had gathered tadpoles in stagnant shallows, and later, caught young frogs under deftly thrown handkerchiefs. She had carried them home in her pockets to make them predict the weather in empty jelly jars fitted with matchstick ladders and covered with gauze. If the frog sat on top of the ladder, the weather would be warm and sunny; if it crouched at the bottom, it would rain. Only, the frogs always sat at the top, trying to get out, until they fell to the bottom, and died.

At last Inge reached the rustic wooden fence around the Waldhaus and its grounds. Under grape arbors, benches and chairs, and tables covered with red and white checkered cloths were waiting for customers. A notice was nailed to the gate. "Under new management," it said. And underneath, in ornate Gothic lettering, "Jews are not welcome here."

- Chapter 8 -

Inge returned home from school the next day, Thursday, excited by the prospect of Elfriede's visit. She had pushed the unpleasant experience in her friend's home to the back of her mind. Oma had left by an early train for Düsseldorf so as to be at the airport in good time. Her daughter Lydia and her family were stopping off a few hours between planes, on the first lap of their journey to the United States of America. From Düsseldorf, they were to fly to London, then go by train to Liverpool where they were to board an ocean liner bound for New York.

Frau Landmann had told Inge some of the details of the emigration. Since Jews were forbidden to take currency out of Germany, Dr. Blumgarten, Lydia's husband, had invested what moneys he could in the latest medical equipment, and shipped it off in advance to the U.S.A. Aunt Lydia had bought clothes and shoes in increasing sizes for their two boys for growing years to come. She had stocked up on brooms and pails, dishcloths and tablecloths, bed linen and towels, washpowders, toilet soap and toothpaste. All available space in the crates of household furnishings she had stuffed with rolls of toilet paper. The Blumgartens planned to live as cheaply as possible in America, until the doctor could pass all the required examinations, and again practice medicine. They had arranged the hurried meeting with

Frau Landmann to cut good-byes to a minimum, believing that this would be less traumatic for the old lady. Lydia Blumgarten hoped that soon, they would be together for good, "over there".

Inge had informed Doris that she was expecting a guest that afternoon. She did not tell her that her grandmother had in fact forbidden her to see this particular visitor, and was waiting nervously in the drawing room when Doris ushered in Elfriede. Inge had not heard the sound of the front door bell.

"She came to the back door," Doris explained with raised eyebrows. She gave Elfriede a little push, and the girl stumbled blushing into the room. Her gums showed in an embarrassed grin.

"Come on," Inge said, jumping up and glaring furiously at Doris, "we'll go to my room. I'll show you my things."

She took Elfriede's hand and pulled her along, brushing by Doris who was leaning against the door jamb, a little smile on her lips. Elfriede exuded a faint odor of boiled cabbage.

Now that she was here, Inge did not know what to do with her guest. She had planned no further than her mere forbidden presence. Elfriede's embarrassment was contagious, and both girls shuffled in silence from one foot to the other.

Finally, at her wits' end for a subject of conversation, Inge asked, "Are you hungry? We could get Doris to make us some sandwiches."

Elfriede shook her head. "Un-hunh," she said, "but thanks all the same."

Chapter 8

Again silence fell. Inge coughed. Elfriede twisted the hem of her green dress in her fingers. She kept looking at the ground before her.

"Look," Inge said in desperation as she pulled the doll Amalia off her bed, "have you ever seen one like this?"

For the first time, Elfriede lifted her eyes and gazed at the doll; she drew in her breath. "Ooooh!" she said. "She's beautiful!" She walked around and around Inge and the doll, then poked out a timid finger, not quite touching Amalia. "Would you... would you let me hold her?" she asked, breathlessly.

Inge pushed the doll into Elfriede's arms.

"Sure. Go ahead." She shrugged.

Elfriede held the doll reverently. Her face was flushed. "Ooooh! How I wish I had a doll like this one!"

"Well, you can't have her. She's mine." Inge yanked Amalia out of the girl's arms and threw her back onto the bed. Elfriede eyes filled with tears, her arms still shaped to cradle the doll.

"Let's get out of here," Inge said. "Come on. Can you climb trees?"

"Uh-hunh," Elfriede shook her head. "It ruins clothes; my Ma wouldn't let me. But... will you show me your house? I've never seen one like it."

"Oh, all right, then. This way." Inge was getting bored with her visitor. Maybe she had made a mistake, after all. Maybe Oma knew what she was talking about.

As she led the way to the library, she asked casually, "Did your brother say anything more after I left, yesterday? About me, I mean?"

SPRING INTO WINTER

"Uh-hunh," Elfriede said again, and Inge began to hate the sound. "He wouldn't have dared, not with our Ma there. Ooooh!" she exclaimed as she looked around, "all those books! Have you read them all?"

Inge laughed. "Of course not," she said. "Don't be silly. They're grown-up books. They belong to my grandmother."

Leather-bound volumes crowded the cherrywood shelves. Poets in matched sets: Goethe, Schiller, and the Jew Heinrich Heine, excerpts of whose works, too-well-known to be left out of anthologies, were now attributed to "author unknown" in school books of German literature. Philosophers such as Kant, Hegel, Schopenhauer, and especially Nietzsche, were abundantly represented on Oma's library shelves.

Inge pulled a thick tome from a set of encyclopedias. She opened it at a brightly colored page and held it out to Elfriede.

"Look," she said, pointing at an anatomical chart of the human male. "That's what a man's thing looks like!" Her face flushed, she glanced over her shoulder at the door. Both girls were breathing fast, their heads touching over the page. Elfriede straightened up.

"I know," she said casually. "I've seen my brother's."

"Have you really?" Inge's voice held new respect. "You mean he let you see it?"

Elfriede shrugged. "Naw, silly. I just saw it, that's all."

Inge slammed the book shut. "It's boring, anyway," she declared. "And I've seen one too. My cousin's." She

Chapter 8

pushed the book back among its mates.

"That's my mother," she said, pointing at the portrait in oils of a pretty young woman in an oval frame.

On one side of the room was a stone fireplace, a red-upholstered rocking chair beside it. A large desk sat near the glass double door that opened onto a vine-covered balcony; on the wall beside it hung an engraving of Goethe's head. The room smelled of old books and polish, leather and warmth. Nice, Inge thought. I've never noticed it before.

"That's all there is here," she said. "Let's go up to the attic."

They went up unnoticed--both Mister and Mrs. Imhoff worked--to the wash kitchen. Inge pointed out the stone washtub.

"This is where I smoke my grandfather's cigars," she said.

"Ooooh, you never!" Elfriede gaped in admiration. "And your grandma lets you?"

"Oh, sure," Inge said grandly. "She says it's a pity to let them go to waste."

"My mom caught me smoking our Willi's cigarettes once," Elfriede said. "I got ever such a whipping!"

They climbed the last steps to the attic. As Elfriede was pressing her nose through the slats of the children's attic--it had been locked again--Inge said, "My sister's just gone to Belgium, you know."

"I didn't know you had a sister. Why did she go?"

Inge shrugged. "Oh... you know...Jews have got to go."

"Will you be going too, then?"

89

"I guess so. Some time. My mother's coming to get me."

"Where's your mom now? Have you got a dad too?"

"Mmmm-mmmm," Inge said. "They're both there too. In Belgium."

"Is she older than you, your sister?"

"Yes. She's seventeen."

"My brother's twenty-four."

"You got any others? A sister maybe?"

"Naw. Just me and him. He says I'm nothing but an accident."

"Why? What kind of accident?"

Elfriede shrugged. Her bony shoulders lifted the frills on her dress into little wings.

"I don't know," she said. "He only says it when he's mad at me."

"Grown-ups!" Inge voiced contempt at their strange and silly ways. "You'll never know what they'll do next."

"Yeah....My Dad says there's going to be a war."

Inge too had heard talk of war from the adults around her. It seemed a thrilling prospect. Young men in field gray uniforms goose-stepping down the streets, the hob-- nails under their boots kicking sparks out of the cobblestones. Singing rousing songs. No matter if those songs advised the citizens to "line the Jews up against the wall!" The martial tunes struck a responding chord in Inge's breast. She loved parades.

"We'll win for sure," she said. "Japan's on our side. If there's a war, the Japanese will help us and then we'll win in no time at all!"

Chapter 8

Elfriede's eyes shone. "They're ever so handsome, the soldiers, aren't they?" she said.

Inge had never noticed the face of a soldier. It was to the uniform that she thrilled, and the face beneath the peaked cap or steel helmet did not register at all.

Changing subjects, she now said, "Let's go downstairs. I want to show you something."

She led Elfriede into her grandmother's bedroom and with a vague gesture, pointed out the white built-in closets.

"My grandmother gave me a huge piece of platinum for my birthday," she said. "It's in there, in her safe."

"What's platinum?"

"It's some precious stuff. Like gold, only it looks like silver."

"Go on! What would she give you that for?"

"It's for the future," Inge said importantly. "It's worth a great deal of money."

"How much?" Elfriede's eyes glittered.

"Oh, I don't know... Maybe a million!"

"Go on! I don't believe you."

"Suit yourself." Inge spread her hands. "I know it's worth a lot of money. My grandmother's very rich!"

"Show it to me, then! Or I won't believe you."

Inge had no idea of the location of Frau Landmann's safe. "I promised not to tell anyone," she said. "So, I won't show it to you."

"You won't because it isn't true!"

"Oh, but it is!"

"It isn't."

"It is, too!"

SPRING INTO WINTER

"All right, show me!"

Inge stamped her foot. She flushed with rage.

"I won't, then! And I don't care if you don't believe me. I'm going downstairs!" She ran out the door, not waiting for Elfriede.

The other girl quickly caught up with her and held her back by an arm. "I was only fooling," she wheedled, "I really believe you, I do! Let's be friends again."

"Oh, all right," Inge agreed. "But you'd better believe what I say, or I won't be your friend anymore."

"What if you tell a lie?"

"I don't lie, ever!" Inge expanded with selfrighteousness. "I have no need to," she added grandly.

The girls jumped down the last three steps of the stairs into the hall. On one side it was lit by multicolored stained-glass windows that followed the staircase, and on another, by the glass folding doors of the reception room. This room had sea-green wall-to-wall carpeting with a pattern of tiny black fleur-de-lys.

The last time that this room had been used, Inge remembered, was a few years ago, at the occasion of her grandfather's seventieth birthday. The family was still complete, and everybody had been present. Aunt Lydia and her husband had come from Berlin with their two sons. Uncle Emil and Aunt Emma still lived across the street, and were there with Dietrich and Miriam, Bernd and Eva. Inge's mother and father were there, and Erika. A photographer had taken pictures of them all grouped in front of the tall bow windows. Inge herself, the youngest grandchild, in an embroidered short white dress, a barrette in her bobbed blonde hair, had been leaning

Chapter 8

against her grandmother's knee.

Now she stood by the folding doors, her forehead pressed against the cold glass. How long ago that seemed, how far away and forever gone, those children and grown-ups who had posed with her for the family portrait.

"Let's go in!" Elfriede whispered in her ear. She had pressed her palms against the glass. Now she removed them, leaving greasy imprints.

Inge shuddered. What did this girl have in common with her? Why had she ever invited her?

"No!" she said, harshly.

"Why not?" Elfriede whined, "I haven't done anything!"

"Never mind, Elfriede. It doesn't matter." Inge was suddenly weary. "This room's only opened for big occasions, like my grandmother's birthday. Last year, my mother was here, too..." She stopped, gulped. She was not going to cry! Not in front of a non-Jew, a Goy!

Frau Landmann came home early that evening. She looked smaller somehow, diminished. Fate had now robbed her of her youngest child as well, of her grandsons. Until then, she had used her walking stick to behead weeds, slap obstructions out of her way, or yank objects within her reach by its crook. Now, she relied heavily on its support. For the first time, Inge found that the ample black garments her grandmother usually wore, really looked black. Her clothes hung on her sadly, as though her body had lost its firmness. Her mouth was slack, like it was after removing her dentures.

Doris had prepared a cold supper on a tray, ready to serve Frau Landmann in the drawing room. But the old lady shook her head.

"Not tonight, thank you, Doris," she said. "I will go straight to bed."

As she walked to the stairs, Frau Landmann's feet seemed to cling to the floor. Inge went to her side in silence and, taking the cane gently from her hand, placed the heavy arm on her own thin shoulders and supported her grandmother up the stairs. It was a slow ascent.

Doris watched until they had reached the landing.

Frau Landmann was silent. She sat down heavily at the edge of her bed, her eyes flat. Inge knelt in front of her, unlaced the sturdy black shoes and gently removed them. Her grandmother's misshapen feet did not even wriggle at the relief. Inge unhooked the old lady's creaking corsets, loosened and braided the thin white hair, and helped her into bed. The silence between them was more eloquent than speech. The bond that tied the child to the old woman was closer than ever. Inge knew that now, she was the only one of their blood in Germany left to her grandmother. As the old lady weakened, her strength flowed into Inge, and made her strong.

As Inge was about to leave the room, Frau Landmann said, "Sit with me a while, child."

Inge returned to the bed and sat on the edge. Oma held out a hand, and Inge took it in both hers and slowly stroked it. The veins were standing thick and blue on its back; they felt soft when she pressed down on them, but sprang up again when she released them. Inge studied the striated old nails, carefully buffed to a hard gloss.

Chapter 8

She looked at her grandmother's face in the failing evening light, saw the old mouth quiver at the corners and tears ooze slowly from the closed lids. How old she has got today, Inge thought. She lifted the heavy hand to her lips and kissed it, and held it against her cheek. A faint pressure of the thick fingers acknowledged the gesture.

Frau Landmann never drew the drapes in her room, and now in the blue of the night, Inge saw the lights of the city sparkle below and far away, as though the Milky Way flowed through the valley. A train whistled in the distance, and in the garden an owl hooted. Oma's tears had stopped, and her hand slackened in Inge's. She laid it back on the quilt and tiptoed out of the room that seemed to swell and contract with the rhythm of the old lady's breathing.

- Chapter 9 -

There was mail again at breakfast. A letter for Frau Landmann with a Belgian stamp, and an official-looking one for Doris, with a German stamp. The young girl looked up radiantly from it.

"It's come!" she said, "I've got it! My visa's been approved, I can go to Palestine!"

Suddenly she pushed away her breakfast plate, laid her arms on the table and, sobbing, buried her face in them.

Frau Landmann, supported by her customary willpower, had learned to cope with her youngest daughter's departure. Encouraging Doris good-naturedly, she chided, "Now, child, this is a time for rejoicing!"

Doris lifted her tear-stained face and looked at the old lady.

"I know," she said, sniffling, "only... only... I didn't really believe I would ever get it!" And she burst into tears again.

Frau Landmann handed her a handkerchief. "There now, girl," she said briskly, "blow your nose and tell us more about it."

Doris groped for the handkerchief and blew into it, then wiped her eyes.

"I can leave at the end of October, on that boat from Hamburg. My father has already booked a passage for me." She sat up and her eyes widened. "Oh!" she said,

Chapter 9

"that means I'll have to... I'll have to..." She stopped.

"You will have to leave us," Frau Landmann finished for her, matter-of-factly. Doris swallowed and nodded. "Well," the old lady went on, "that was to be expected, sooner or later. There now," she added as a fresh flood of tears was starting, "stop it! We are happy for you. Very happy!" She turned to Inge. "Aren't we?" she demanded.

Inge had been thinking that she would have to take care of the shopping again. She hung her head.

"Inge?" her grandmother prompted. "We *are* glad at Doris's good luck, are we not?"

Inge stared at the napkin in her lap. "We are happy for you, Doris," she muttered.

When she looked up at her grandmother, she noticed the old lady's hand still holding the knife she had used to open the envelope. The letter was still unread.

"Oma," she said, "you haven't read your mail yet."

She had recognized the scrawl of her mother's writing.

Frau Landmann had been looking at Inge with a frown. Now she glanced down at the letter in her hand as though surprised and said:

"That's right. Well, let's see what your mother has to say." She unfolded the closely-written pages, crackling the paper.

Frau Landmann read in silence, her lips pressed into a thin line. Inge watched her expectantly. She tried to read a meaning from her grandmother's expression, but the old lady's features remained non-committal. At last, she looked at Inge over her glasses and, tapping the letter with a finger, she said, "So. Erika made it. She arrived in excellent health." Frau Landmann chuckled. "Your mother is upset because the girl has got so fat," she went on. "Now she is blaming Lydia that she let it happen. Poor Lydia!"

Oma put the letter down beside her plate and concentrated on buttering a roll, then drank some coffee. "I could have told your mother how it happened. It wasn't Lydia's fault, not in any way....Lydia," she stopped and her mouth quivered a little. She sat up straighter in her chair and went on firmly, "Lydia told me on the telephone that after your sister had left, she found piles of fudge and toffee wrappers between the girl's bed and the wall." Frau Landmann laughed. "And your aunt had wondered why Erika was never hungry at table, and yet got fatter by the day!" The old lady shook with laughter. "Glands, she thought it was. Glands!" She wiped her eyes with her napkin. "I'll have to tell your mother. What a brood!"

"Is that all?" Inge asked. She was not amused. In the old days, Erika had constantly bullied her, and Inge didn't care whether Erika was fat or thin.

Frau Landmann picked up the letter again.

"I haven't finished reading," she said. "Your mother has the most awful handwriting. She should get herself a typewriter!" She trailed off as her eyes swept slowly over the lines.

Some time ago, Frau Landmann herself, in response to complaints that her handwriting had become illegible, had bought a second-hand typewriter. She now typed her letters, clumsily and with many typos, using her two forefingers.

Chapter 9

Frau Landmann checked in her reading, went back over the text. Quickly she glanced at Inge, lowered her eyes again.

It was nearly time for school; the tram was due soon. Inge slid impatiently from side to side on her chair.

"What's the matter?" Oma asked. "Got an itch?"

Inge blushed. She shook her head and said, "The tram's nearly due and you haven't told me anything yet."

"Your mother's coming home middle of next month," Frau Landmann said brusquely, then her face broadened in a smile.

"Yippee!" Inge jumped up--her chair nearly tipped over backwards--and raced around the table. She flung her arms around Oma's neck and hugged her extravagantly. The old lady gasped for air and struggled out of the embrace.

"Whoa!" she said, taking a deep breath. "Gently does it! Now run and catch your tram. It's another month till she comes!"

Inge danced out of the dining room on pillows of air. Mutti, she thought, it's been so long! Will you know me? I have grown up since you saw me last. I'm ten years old! Her face crumpled: and you did not even remember my birthday.

During supper that evening, Frau Landmann was unusually silent. And later when, her homework done, Inge came into the drawing room to kiss her good-night, Oma held her back.

"Sit down, Inge," she said, "there's something I have to tell you."

SPRING INTO WINTER

Inge perched on the arm of her grandmother's chair. Frau Landmann sighed.

"This morning, I did not tell you everything your mother wrote," she said at last. "When she comes, next month, it's to take you away with her."

Inge jumped down. "You mean I'll be going to Belgium?" Oma had waited all day to tell her--how could she!

Frau Landmann nodded. "Pleased?" she asked, with a little smile.

Inge paced up and down. She beat her fists together softly, then started chewing her thumbnail. "How about you?" she asked, stopping in front of her grandmother.

"What *about* me?"

"Well, will you be coming with us?"

Frau Landmann shook her head. "You first," she said.

"Then I won't go. I'm not going without you."

"My dear child, you'll do as you are told. Besides, I'll need more time here, to sell the house and so on."

"But you can't stay here alone! Doris will be gone too!"

The old lady shrugged. "I'm not completely helpless, you know. And then there are the Imhoffs, upstairs."

"They're no use!"

"They are good people. *And* they happen to be living here. So I won't be alone, you see."

Inge stopped in front of her grandmother and glared at her with hot eyes. "I won't have it!" she said. "And if my mother knew, she would insist," the unfamiliar word made her lisp, "she would insist that you come, too."

Chapter 9

Frau Landmann leaned back in her chair and looked up at her granddaughter.

"My, but you are taking a lot upon yourself!" she mocked. Then she grabbed Inge's hand and pulled her down. "Come and sit on my lap and we'll talk this over calmly."

At first, Inge resisted, sitting stiffly on Oma's lap, but then gave in to the comfort of the familiar shape and snuggled up, adapting her own body to the old lady's soft contours. Frau Landmann stroked Inge's silky hair. Her hand shook a little.

"Now then," Oma began, "you must realize that your mother is taking a great risk in coming to get you. A very great risk."

"Why?" Inge asked, stiffening. "She hasn't done anything wrong!"

"Don't be stupid, child. You know well enough that any Jew who comes here is at risk. And now listen to me, and don't interrupt. Your mother has obtained your visa--heaven only knows how much she had to pay--but it's for a limited time only, on her passport." Inge stirred, and Oma tightened her hold. "So she'll get here one day, and go off with you the next."

Frau Landmann paused, while her hand went on mechanically stroking Inge's hair. "I have applied for a visa as well," she continued, "but I haven't heard anything yet. Until I do, I can't make a firm decision." She gave Inge a playful slap on the rear. "And now, off to bed with you. As I said before, I'll need more time here, anyway, to wind things up."

SPRING INTO WINTER

Inge threw her arms around Oma's neck. "I don't want you to sell our house," she cried. "It's *our* house! I don't want a stranger living here! And... and... I don't want to leave you!"

Her thin body shook with sobs. Her chest ached. Her mind churned and churned with grief, but she was totally oblivious to Oma's possible pain.

"There now. There, there," Frau Landmann whispered, "it isn't as bad as all that. We'll soon be together again, you'll see..." She cleared her throat and continued more firmly, "And now, to bed with you, young lady. It's long past your bedtime."

That night Inge cried herself to sleep. Her mouth felt dry and sour, her lips stuck together as though they would never open again in speech.

In the weeks that followed, Inge got accustomed to the thought of leaving. She looked around her greedily, with wonder, knowing that she was saying good-bye. Everything she knew and loved became an indelible imprint on her memory; she gathered and stored impressions. She would pass questing fingers over the roughness of a stucco wall, meeting with delight some sudden smoothness. She would rub her cheek against the bark of a cherry tree and taste in memory the tartness of the fruit, see in her mind's eye its bright red translucence. She caught the scent of apples ripening in a neighbor's garden, and the sweet pungency of horse manure spread on vegetable beds. The peace of the misty mornings as she stood waiting for the tram that would take her into the valley wrung her heart with a foretaste of nostalgia.

Chapter 9

Doris also was getting ready to leave. Her happy singing filled the house. Her work improved a hundredfold; she wanted to leave behind her a memory of perfection. She was brimming with kindness toward Inge, laughed at her every quip. It seemed that Inge could do no wrong, however hard she tried.

By the beginning of October, the creeping vine that clung to the front and side of the house had turned blood red. On Monday 10, when Inge came home from school, she found Frau Landmann waiting on the look-out bench. The old lady was wrapped in a woolen shawl that she held close to her neck with clumsy fingers. The cold she felt did not seem altogether due to the chill autumn air.

"Don't go in yet, Inge," she said. "There's something I must tell you first."

Inge sat down close to her grandmother and snuggled up to her. She shivered .

"It's cold out here, Oma," she complained.

"Doris has had bad news," the old lady said over Inge's head. "I want you to be specially kind to her."

Inge swallowed and sat up. She gazed fearfully at her grandmother, waiting.

"They made a new law yesterday," Frau Landmann went on. She was silent for a little, as though she found it beyond her strength to continue.

"What they've done," she said at last, "is to invalidate our passports for foreign travel."

"What does that mean?" Inge asked, puzzled.

"It means, Inge, that no Jew can now legally leave the country."

"But she's got her visa, Oma. Doris has got her visa!"

That word, visa, was as familiar to Jews in Hitler's Germany as "car" or "hot dog" to Americans. It had, from necessity, become an everyday topic of conversation.

Frau Landmann nodded. "So she has, Inge. But her visa's no use to her now, because her passport has become invalid."

Inge ached with sympathy to her very fingertips.

"Poor Doris," she whispered, "what's she going to do now? She was so looking forward to Palestine."

"I know." Suddenly, Frau Landmann sat up. She slammed her left fist into her right palm. Her shawl slipped from her shoulders. "The swine!" she spat. "It's damnable! The diabolical, fiendish, bastardly swine!"

Inge leaned over and adjusted her grandmother's shawl. "You mustn't catch cold," she said. Then a thought struck her. "Oma, what about us? I have a visa, and what about your passport?"

"No use, child. No use at all."

"But my mother! She is coming to get me! Does that mean that now...?"

"It seems there is one way out. If you can get the signature of the Minister of the Interior." Frau Landmann laughed bitterly. "Somebody's going to make a fortune!"

"So if Doris got that signature from the Minister of what'd you-call-it, she'd be all right?"

"She would, I suppose. But I can tell you right now that it's going to be hard to obtain, *very* hard."

"And if she can't get it, she'll have to stay in Germany?"

Chapter 9

Deep down, Inge could not help wishing that Doris would have to stay. That way she, Inge, would not have to start shopping again. She was immediately ashamed of her selfishness.

"That's right. Unless she can manage to get out the 'black' way." Frau Landmann mused in silence. "Black," like "visa," had become part of every Jew's vocabulary. It meant buying "under the table," illegally--at a considerable cost--something that until recently had been available perfectly legally. The old lady set her cane to the ground and, helped by Inge, levered herself up. Moving heavily toward the front door she said, "I should think that it would be very difficult to get a 'black' passage on a boat to the Middle East. Yes."

Inge danced impatiently around the old lady.

"What about us, Oma? What about us?"

"We'll see. Something's got to be worked out. After all, your sister managed to get out without papers. We'll be sure to think of something."

"Do you think my mother won't be coming, now?"

Frau Landmann pinched Inge's cheek and smiled down at her. "I'm sure she'll find a way," she said. As she draped her shawl over a brass coathanger in the cloakroom she added, "I must tell you, though, that I think she'd be crazy to come back at this time."

"Why? She has to come and get me, hasn't she?"

"Crazy. She might not be able to get out again."

"But Oma..."

Inge's mouth quivered. At last she had come to terms with the thought of her departure. Was she going to be forced to stay here, after all?

- Chapter 10 -

Doris did not come down for supper that night, and at breakfast the next morning, she was pale, her eyes red-rimmed. Frau Landmann and Inge avoided looking at her, not to embarrass her in her grief. The day was gray, and as though in sympathy, rain fell steadily.

At school, Herr Bauer's face wore a more than usually malevolent smirk.

"So," he hissed close to Inge's ear as he limped past, "we'll get you yet!'

Inge kept her eyes riveted on her book and showed no response. The teacher moved on. Whenever he looked in her direction, Herr Bauer rubbed his hands together with a dry rasping sound. How could he be so dry, with all that rain? Inge thought.

All that day it rained. The earth and the very air soaked up moisture to the point of saturation, and by the time Inge came home, water was gurgling down the stone steps to the garden below. Raindrops ran races down the windowpanes. The steady sound of rushing water filled the house from attic to cellar.

Doris retired early. She seemed to have no wish for company. She would write to her friend in Palestine, she said, and hope that the letter would reach him.

Chapter 10

After supper, Inge and her grandmother sat together at the drawing room table. Frau Landmann was teaching Inge to play rummy, a new game for her. A porcelain table lamp with a tasseled silk shade shed its light on the white head and the blond one. As she dealt the cards, the old lady's hands made pale patterns against the Oriental rug that covered the table.

It was dark outside, wet and cold, and the house gave peace and shelter. At nine o'clock, just before Inge's bedtime, the doorbell jangled.

Frau Landmann and Inge looked at each other, startled.

"Whoever could that be, at this hour?" Inge whispered.

Frau Landmann licked her lips. She laid a hand over Inge's. "We don't have to answer," she said.

They waited in silence, with scared eyes. The doorbell rang again, longer.

"Shall we..." Inge said, "I mean, shouldn't we see who...?"

The old lady stood up awkwardly. "Come with me, but stay out of sight," she said.

They tiptoed through the dark lobby. Inge held on to her grandmother's dress and stayed behind her. At the moment of turning on the porch light from the foyer, the bell sounded again. Inge and the old lady froze.

The porch light threw onto the stained glass of the door the huge neckless silhouette of a man. He stood there, motionless. Taking a deep breath and releasing it, Frau Landmann opened the door without removing the security chain.

"What do you want?" she asked through the crack.

The man whipped the cap off his head and in the lamplight, his hair was haloed with moisture.

"The name's Flasche, Ma'am," he said. "You don't know me, but our Elfriede's a friend of your little girl."

"What's this?" Frau Landmann hauled the confused Inge from behind her. "Didn't I forbid you...?"

"Don't blame the little girl, Ma'am, kids will be kids." The man's voice was deep and husky. Now he looked over his shoulder as though making sure he was alone. "Would you mind letting me in, just for a moment?" he asked.

When the old lady did not reply, he added, "You needn't be afraid, really you needn't."

Frau Landmann shrugged. Nothing risked, nothing gained, the gesture seemed to say. She slid the security chain out of its groove and opened the door. At the same time, she switched off the porch light, and the foyer light on.

Closing the door softly behind him, the man cleaned his shoes methodically on the doormat. He was dressed in dark pants and pullover. He was wearing no coat, and his shoulders were black from the rain. He wiped his nose on the back of his hand, apologizing.

"You must forgive me, Ma'am, for coming at this hour of the night," he said. "But it wouldn't do for me to be seen."

His lean cheeks were furrowed from nose to mouth, and when he spoke, he showed strong yellow teeth with a gap at the upper left. It was a reassuring face, somehow. Frau Landmann motioned with her hand toward

Chapter 10

the hall.

"Won't you come in, Herr Flasche."

"Thank you, Ma'am."

The old lady led the way into the drawing room, switching off lights as she went. When she sat down in her armchair, Inge leaned close to her side. Herr Flasche hesitated in the doorway, shifting his weight from one foot to the other.

"Come in, come in," Frau Landmann said. "Take a seat."

The man entered and sat down at the edge of a straight chair. He held his cap in his hands and turned it over and over, frowning down at it as though it were some strange object the secret of which he was trying to fathom. He coughed, then looked up suddenly. Frau Landmann's and Inge's eyes were fixed on him in silent inquiry.

"Frau Landmann, Ma'am," Herr Flasche said, and coughed again, "I am truly sorry, and so is Frau Flasche, for all the trouble you people are having." He cleared his throat. The old lady waited. "You must not think that all us Aryans...that all Germans are like that." He blushed deeply and mopped his brow with his cap.

Frau Landmann smiled. "I am happy to hear you say that, Herr Flasche," she said. "Though I must admit that it strikes me as strange, coming from you."

Herr Flasche frowned down at his boots. "You'll be thinking of my son," he said.

The old lady nodded. "Yes. I have heard that you have a boy in the S.A."

SPRING INTO WINTER

Inge shifted. How did Oma know this, she wondered. Frau Landmann looked around at her.

"Isn't it past your bedtime?" she asked.

"Please let me stay up, Oma! Please!"

Frau Landmann glanced at her visitor. He was smiling at Inge.

"Our Elfriede likes you, a lot," he said. "She told me of your visits together."

"I'll have your explanation of this later, young lady," Frau Landmann said. "For now, you may stay-- five minutes longer."

"What I came to say is this, Ma'am." Herr Flasche moved his feet and his boots squeaked as they rubbed against each other. "Excuse me," Herr Flasche said, reddening.

"Well, what is it that you came to tell me?" Frau Landmann tried to sound encouraging.

"I know it sounds bad, our Willi in the S.A. and all. But you must believe me, Frau Landmann, when I tell you that he joined up against our wishes, his mother's and mine." Again Herr Flasche studied his cap. "You don't have much control over your children, these days," he added softly.

Frau Landmann nodded and shot a quick telling glance at Inge, who fidgeted uncomfortably.

"Ma'am, I came to tell you that I want to help you. Whenever I can be of use. In whatever way."

Frau Landmann was silent. Then, groping for Inge's hand, she rose stiffly from her chair and crossed over to her visitor. She held out her right hand and the man, standing up, shyly took it.

Chapter 10

"Herr Flasche," the old lady said, and her voice shook a little, "I don't know what to say. I am very... I am deeply touched. Thank you." She halted, pondering. "I know that you ran a great risk coming here, and I appreciate it. But as a policeman, you stand to lose your job if it were ever found out that you...that you..."

"Some of us feel, Ma'am, that 'they' should not get it all their own way. And we are prepared to take risks." Herr Flasche mopped his face with his cap. "Just keep it in mind, Frau Landmann, Ma'am. You and your little one here," he smiled down at Inge, "you two still have friends in this town." He walked to the door. "I'd best be going now, if you don't mind."

Frau Landmann accompanied him to the door and again shook hands with him. Then he disappeared into the hissing, gurgling night.

Back in the drawing room, the old lady sat in her chair and dropped her hands into her lap.

"Well," she said, "who would have believed it. And from that kind of person, yet." She looked up at Inge who was braiding the tassels of the lampshade. "Inge," Frau Landmann said, "there are some decent Gentiles left in Germany, after all!"

On and on it rained. The clouds seemed to have stopped above the valley and kept on pouring unlimited gallons of water onto the saturated ground. The river swelled, reached near-flood levels. The burning colors of autumn were washed into uniform browns and grays. Everywhere, the sound of gurgling, swishing, dripping rain. And there was not much comfort in the house. The damp pervaded the very carpets that covered the floors.

Frau Landmann was reluctant to start the furnace. She wanted to save for the coldest days of winter the little reserve of coal she had. She and Inge went about in several layers of clothes. The old lady knitted remnants of wool into striped multicolored socks for Inge, mostly dark brown, navy, or black. Not one sock had a matching mate, and Inge hated them all with equal passion. But she had to wear them, and even her feet were sulking.

Doris had applied to the Minister of the Interior for ratification of her passport. While she waited for a decision, she went about her tasks in silence. Her crisp red hair lost its bounce, and she did not bother to keep up her appearance. Her life now seemed to be but a breath between one mail delivery and the next.

Inge dragged herself to school and back. Since the latest edict, there had been no news from her mother. Then, on the fifteenth, a Saturday, a letter came. It was the very weekend that Frau Richter had intended to come and pick up her daughter.

Frau Landmann read the letter to Inge upon her return from school that afternoon.

"'You must know how terrible I feel about this new edict,'" the old lady read. "'But unless I can be sure that I can leave the country again, I am not going to set foot in it. It would not be fair to Hans and Erika. Don't worry, though, I promise that I shall come and get you, my darling Inge. You must just be patient a little while longer. I know that you are going to do your best to help Oma in these difficult times, until I come for you.'"

Chapter 10

Frau Landmann blew her nose. Inge's lower lip jutted and her eyes stung with unshed tears.

She crossed over to the window and leaned her forehead against the pane, gazing at the dripping gray world outside. Soon, she did not know where the rain stopped and her tears began.

Frau Landmann studied the thin childish shape outlined against the dull light, and sighed.

"Let's see now. Where was I? Ah, here we are." She cleared her throat and resumed reading. "'If I cannot obtain official permission to come back, and assurances that I can get out again, I shall find another way. In any case, let me assure both of you that I will come. It will have to be a little later than I had hoped, say another week or two.'"

Frau Richter went on to describe living conditions in Brussels, and the weather. She seemed to like the city, and thought that Inge would, too. For the time being, the little family was living in two furnished rooms, with use of bath and kitchen.

"'As soon as Hans's contacts have sent more business his way, we shall move into larger quarters,'" Inge's mother continued. "'He has already met several people here who knew him in the old days, who are willing to help him find his footing. You know what a hard worker he is, Mother. He is sure to succeed. And then we shall make your life here very comfortable. I can hardly wait for that day.'"

Frau Landmann addressed Inge's back. "Are you listening, child?"

SPRING INTO WINTER

Inge nodded, her head bumping the windowpane. She had jammed her fists into the pockets of her sweater, where they made it bulge, pulling it out of shape. She squinted at the twin disks of steam on the glass, that grew and shrank with her breathing.

"Go on," she said tonelessly, "I am listening."

"Come over here, where I can see you. And I'll tell you what," the old lady said. "When I've finished reading you this letter--it's on the long side!--what do you say we go to the kitchen and I make you a nice cup of hot chocolate? And we'll bake a cake!" She sat back and smiled encouragingly at Inge. "Well, what do you think?"

Cheered, Inge turned back into the room. The prospect of a treat straightened her shoulders and put color in her cheeks. She switched on the table lamp on her way to her grandmother.

"It's getting dark, Oma." Her voice had a lift to it. "You'll ruin your eyes, reading in the dark."

"Oh, my eyes..." The old lady sighed. "They'll last long enough for what remains to be seen....But you are right, child. It is getting dark. The days are drawing in. Well, what about that cake?"

"May I make it by myself?"

"Well... we'll see. First let's finish this letter."

Inge settled herself on the arm of her grandmother's chair and leaned against her, searching her warmth. Frau Landmann tucked her arm around the child, and drew her close. She held the letter in the other hand and, after giving Inge a quick kiss, went on reading.

"'Do you remember the Seligmanns from Hanover?'"

Chapter 10

"Do I ever!" Inge interrupted. "They have a horrid boy, Bob, he always pulled my hair and punched me, when they came to visit. And a large dog, Teddy."

"I can't say that I remember them, but since you do... Now don't interrupt again." Frau Landmann searched for the place where she had stopped and went on. "'They have been here a couple of years already, and are doing very well. They have been very kind to us, have had us over for dinner twice.'" Frau Landmann leaned back and crossed her arms on the shelf of her bosom.

"I cannot understand your mother," she said. "Has it come to this, that she needs this...this condescension? Kind indeed! A handout! To *my* daughter!"

"But Oma, you knew! You've read the letter before, haven't you?"

"Of course I have. But this bit here," she tapped the offending passage with a knuckle, "this bit makes me wild all over again. I cannot stand *meekness*! I cannot understand how your mother can be so... so *humble*!"

Inge giggled nervously, and the old lady went on, "Come to think of it, I think I do know those people. Seligmann." She turned to Inge. "Wasn't *she* born a Lazar?"

"How should I know?"

"Yes. I'm sure that's who they are. Lazar! Why, the upstarts! Her father was nothing but a kosher butcher!"

Inge wriggled. She had never met a kosher butcher. The only butcher she knew was Herr Fritsche, and she rather liked him.

"Is it bad, being a kosher butcher?" she asked.

"There is nothing wrong with being a kosher butcher, child. *If* you know your place. But that kind of people often come from Poland, or Rumania, or some place like that. They are ambitious, and they are never satisfied till they can lord it over us!"

Inge tried to puzzle this out. She had been brought up in the belief that Eastern European Jews were inherently inferior to German Jews. But she had once met a boy who was a Polish Jew, and try as she might, she had found him no different from her other acquaintances. Rather nice, in fact. When she had questioned her grandmother, the old lady had simply forbidden her to play with that boy again. So it was a delicate subject, Inge realized, and she avoided it. It was easiest to come back to her mother's letter.

"Oma," she asked, "what sort of things do they eat in Belgium?"

"Raw horses," came Frau Landmann's pat reply.

"Oma! I mean, *really*?"

"Oh, I think they eat pretty well. They all look fat enough! I've been there only once, years ago. In Knocke, it was, by the sea. And they do eat raw horse, smoked. It's called 'Filet d'Anvers,' and it's absolutely delicious."

Inge shuddered.

"Something like our raw smoked ham," the old lady explained. "And they have little yellow shops on wheels, where they sell French fried potatoes. Fried in horse fat."

"Ugh!" Inge said. "Did you eat any?"

"Hmmm-mmmm!" Frau Landmann nodded. "It gives them that special flavor. How to describe it....It's, well,

Chapter 10

it's just a *Belgian* flavor. Rich. You'll love it. Also, they have the most beautiful carthorses in the world. Brabanters."

"They the ones they *eat*?"

"I don't know....Maybe when they are old and useless, like me."

"You're not old and useless! How can you say that?"

"Well...I *am* old, there's no getting around that." Frau Landmann lumbered to her feet and pulled Inge after her. "However," she said, "I suppose I am still able to do my bit....Let's go bake that cake now!"

- Chapter 11 -

Cold and wet, the days dragged on. Once in a while, the clouds parted on a sky washed nearly white, and an anemic sun shone briefly. It was unusual weather for October, as November was the month for rain and fog. Colds were the order of the day. Some scholarship girls at the Lyzeum, Irmgard among them, would hide in their pockets or sleeves handkerchiefs made from old sheets beyond repair. Most schoolgirl noses, however, were delicately dabbed with the right kind of linen square.

Many pupils were absent, and the school echoed to the coughs and sneezes of those who were not. The number of teachers also shrank, and the missing ones had to be replaced by substitutes. Herr Bauer however seemed germ-resistant, his complexion no yellower than usual, and his lips as purple. He seemed to resent the fact that Inge also had withstood the onslaught of the prevailing misery. He circled her menacingly with his uneven step and yelled into her ear, "Blow your crooked nose, Sarah Richter!"

Inge obligingly dabbed at her dry nose with her handkerchief and shrugged imperceptibly. She had become used to the man's venom and it touched her hardly at all. This very indifference made the teacher foam and sputter with rage. Inge amused herself with a mental image of Herr Bauer performing a wild dance like Rumpelstiltskin in the fairy tale, until in a paroxysm of fury

Chapter 11

he stamped right through the wooden floor and disappeared in a cloud of sulfur.

The teacher of Nature Studies came down with the flu, and a substitute was sent to take her place. This was the young woman's first visit to the Lyzeum, and she gazed nervously at the horde of little girls staring silently back at her. She was tall and slender, and wore her corn-colored braids twisted into a crown around her head. When she addressed the class, she blushed, folding her hands tightly, as in prayer, till her knuckles showed white.

"I am Fräulein Fischer," she said in a soft voice, "and I am sure that you and I will get on famously."

She stopped, looking around expectantly. The girls sat in their benches without moving. A few feet scraped the floor.

"Well now," Fräulein Fischer went on, "I know that so far, you have had no instruction in Racial Studies, which is part of your Nature Studies program this year."

Some girls nodded.

"It's really quite simple," the teacher said. "For the time being, we shall concern ourselves only with three types: the Germanic, the Slavic, and the... er... Semitic."

The girls' interest was kindled. Feet scuffed the floor more vigorously, a few children giggled, nudged each other.

"To show you what I mean by the simplicity of the distinction," Fräulein Fischer said, "I will give you a demonstration."

She strolled through the class, peering closely at the girls' heads as she passed. She touched Inge on the shoulder, and Irmgard Lumpe, and the stocky red-haired girl who had spat in Inge's face on the first day after summer vacation.

"You three go up front and face the class."

Fräulein Fischer shepherded them to the raised platform, then sat down at the desk and studied the seating chart.

"So," she said, and smiled. "You are Irmgard Lumpe." She touched the girl's hand. "And you," nodding at the redhead," are Marianne Pfeiffer. And you, Ingeborg Richter."

The girls smiled back at her nervously. She was so friendly, so pretty, like the girl on the poster with a sheaf of wheat and cornflowers in her arms, advertising work on the farm for the good of Germany. She was like a bit of sunshine on this gray, wet day.

The teacher lined the girls up, Inge first, then Marianne, and Irmgard at the end. Then she proceeded to point out the particular features of each.

"Pay attention now. Ingeborg, here, has a high forehead, narrow cheekbones. Her eyes are blue, the hair smooth and blond. The complexion is fair. The nose, straight. Turn your head, Ingeborg."

Puzzled, Inge complied. What on earth is the teacher getting at, she wondered.

"Look at the back of the head, girls: narrow and elongated." Fräulein Fischer gave Inge a little push and motioned for Marianne to come forward.

"Marianne's forehead is low and rather broad. Her eyes are blue as well, like Ingeborg's." Marianne scowled. "The nose is blunt, and the hair on the coarse side. Now

Chapter 11

turn your head, Marianne." The girl did as she was told. "See this shape?" the teacher said, "Broad, and the neck is short."

Fräulein Fischer turned to Irmgard. "Now you, dear. Would you come forward?"

Irmgard stepped up to the teacher.

"Irmgard here, I would say, is not exactly typical, but enough to point out the differences. Forehead, rather high, but narrow. The cheekbones pronounced, the eyes... the eyes, well, blue. The nose slightly arched. Complexion, sallow."

Irmgard blushed. She was beginning to understand. Fräulein Fischer had been told that there was a Jew in the class, but not *who* she was.

"The hair is straight," the teacher went on. "It is more often apt to be crinkly." She turned back to the class who were watching her, spellbound.

"Here, then, we have our three basic racial types." The teacher motioned the three girls forward. Indicating Inge, she said, "This is a typical Germanic specimen."

From the girls rose a sound like the sea breaking on a rocky shore. They whispered to each other behind their hands and giggled. One or two guffawed, then quickly hushed when Fräulein Fischer clapped her hands sharply.

"Silence, girls! I have not finished!"

A few snorts broke the difficult silence. Inge felt sorry for the teacher.

"Marianne," Fräulein Fischer went on a little uncertainly, "Marianne has Slavic characteristics, although I would not call her *pure* Slavic." Noting the scowl on the girl's face, she smiled at her and said, "There is no reason whatsoever to feel ashamed. A great many good Germans have the same characteristics. After all, our influence has reached far to the east."

As she pulled the reluctant Irmgard forward, the noise in the class broke loose.

"Girls!" Fräulein Fischer clapped her hands again, to no avail. "Girls! A little courtesy, I beg you!"

The girls were beyond quelling. The teacher rapped the desk with a ruler. She flushed angrily.

"I *will* have silence!"

Laughter was bottled up at the cost of watering eyes and running noses. Inge and Irmgard did not dare look at each other. Inge stood with her left foot on her right one, to stop herself from jumping up and down.

"Now," Fräulein Fischer went on, "Irmgard Lumpe here is *not* a typical example of the Semitic race, but she will do."

Irmgard had started to sob quietly behind her cupped hands. The girls shrieked and howled with glee. A rhythmic stamping began, increased in volume and intensity until the floorboards heaved and shuddered. Fräulein Fischer stood helpless by her desk. She had laid an arm protectively around Irmgard's shaking shoulders. Marianne, shrugging, left the platform, and Inge tugged at the teacher's sleeve, desperate to attract her attention. The noise was like a waterfall in a cave.

At last, Inge succeeded in reaching Fräulein Fischer. Pointing first to Irmgard, then to herself, she explained the mistake in frantic whispers. The young teacher turned pale, then red. She looked about her like a trapped

Chapter 11

animal, then fled headlong out of the door. The slap-slap of her low-heeled shoes left ever-decreasing echoes in the empty passages. Behind her, pandemonium spilled from the classroom like marbles from a burst bag. Only the formidable arrival of Herr Doktor Gretz was able to put a stop to it.

The unusual lesson at school had left Inge breathless with exhilaration. Frau Landmann, upon hearing the story, had rocked and roared with laughter, then spent what seemed like hours on the telephone, recounting the incident with increasing embellishments to her friends and acquaintances. She took a particular delight in calling up those of her Gentile friends who had lately curtailed their contact with her, to point out to them the intrinsic stupidity of their Aryan concepts. The old lady was as proud of Inge as if the child had caused the teacher's mistake by some superlative scholastic achievement.

Sometimes, the days of her life appeared to Inge as a see-saw. Up and down, up and down. Lately, the 'down' periods tended to last longer than the 'up' ones. And whenever Inge was happily aloft, there would be the not-to-be-ignored fear that soon, she would come swooping down again, faster than she liked. Thus, none of her pleasures were flawless, just as none of her frustrations had the power to keep her low for long. When a letter arrived from Brussels on the first of November, bearing bad news, Inge was only mildly surprised.

The letter was in Herr Richter's handwriting, a very unusual occurrence. While trying to clean from the outside the kitchen window of their second-floor apartment, Inge's mother had stepped on a skylight invisible under a thick layer of grime, and crashed through the glass to the tiled passage below. She had broken a rib, and her left leg in two places. She was laid up at home, her leg in a plaster cast, her chest tightly bandaged, and thus was unable to come to pick up Inge. God only knew how long she would be out of commission--none of us are getting any younger, Herr Richter added gratuitously.

Frau Landmann was furious. She paced about the drawing room, her ankle-length black dress swishing, and belabored the Turkish rug with her cane. She waved her son-in-law's letter in a vehement fist.

"That silly girl always had a *thing* about cleanliness!" she fumed, as Inge huddled in a corner of the sofa chewing a thumbnail. She tried to imagine her mother as 'that silly girl,' but could only visualize the yellowed photograph of a beautiful child in a dress of Scottish plaid, leaning on a rolled-up sunshade and wearing a large-brimmed hat far back on her long blond hair. Her face was sweet, not silly.

"Nobody ever cleaned a thing to her satisfaction!" Frau Landmann ranted. "No! She paid the maids good money to keep her house in perfect order--perfect!" She shook the letter, now crumpled, under Inge's nose. Inge tittered. "And then," Frau Landmann went on, "she had to go after them, doing everything they had done all over again. Not once, not twice, but every single blessed day!"

Inge well remembered her mother's constant probing for specks of dust. That was just part of Mutti, and as such, to her daughter an unremarkable mannerism. Frau

Chapter 11

Landmann was snorting like an irritated horse, and she dug her cane viciously into the blameless rug.

"What I want to know, and I asked her over and over, 'Paula,' I asked, 'what *do* you pay the girls for?'" The old lady fairly threw herself into her armchair. "I'll tell you," she said, shaking a thick forefinger at Inge, "your mother ought to have her *brain* in a plaster cast, not her leg!"

Inge burst out laughing, but quickly covered the sound by sniffing loudly.

"Blow your nose, child!" Frau Landmann bellowed. "Where's your handkerchief?"

Inge pretended to search her sweater pockets, lifted her shoulders and shook her head. The old lady sighed in exasperation.

"I don't know what the world is coming to," she said. "Manners gone to the devil, no wonder things have come to this pass. Here. Take mine." She threw it at Inge, who caught it.

Inge dabbed at her nose and handed the handkerchief back to her grandmother. Then she went to perch on the arm of the old lady's chair and blew gently into the soft white hair, puffing it up, then patting it back in place. Frau Landmann looked up at Inge and tried a smile. It came out crooked.

"What's going to happen now, Oma?"

Frau Landmann shook her head, wrapped an arm around Inge. "I don't know," she said. "I really do not know. We'll just have to sit here and wait, I suppose. Maybe your mother can think up another of her long-range schemes, or some sort of an arrangement." Suddenly, she sat up straight and rammed her cane onto the floor between her feet. "'Arrangements'!" she snorted. "Why, the silly, innocent little fool!"

"Mutti didn't break her leg on purpose, I'm sure," Inge said mildly.

"I know she didn't, did I say she did? But couldn't she have waited till after she'd got you out?"

Inge shrugged. When Oma got into one of her rages, she felt that their roles were reversed: *she* was the grown-up, and Oma, the child. It was best not to argue with her. She slipped off the chair and sauntered towards the window. The early night was painting the gray sky deep blue. Inge crammed her fists into her pockets and whistled tunelessly between her teeth.

"Come back here!" Frau Landmann commanded.

Inge turned back into the room and came to stand in front of her grandmother. The old lady took one of Inge's hands into her own and peered into her face. Inge kept her eyes down. A little smile lifted the corners of her mouth.

"You seem to be taking all this very calmly?" The old lady was suspicious.

Again Inge shrugged. She withdrew her hand. "Something was bound to happen," she said. She gazed into the watery blue eyes before her. "I had a feeling... What I mean, it was just too good to be true. Mutti coming, I mean, and my going, and... and so on."

She turned back towards the window, then changed her mind, waved a hand limply at her grandmother, and left the room. She bumped against the door frame without noticing. Then she went to the library, sat motionless

Chapter 11

in the rocking chair and stared unseeing into the night. The room was unlit, and in the dark, the once-wonderful learned scent of old leather and printed paper took on an acrid, sinister character. Unblinking, Inge thought of nothing--a great black void too vast even to have a rim from which to topple into it.

At supper, Inge ate mechanically and in silence, without tasting her food. She did not notice Oma's and Doris's--poor pale ghost--attempts to draw her into conversation. But Frau Landmann believed that, as long as a child ate a normal amount of food, all was well; and so she did not insist.

That night, Inge had a dream. She was looking for her mother in a house full of passages lined with doors. She was opening door after door, hopelessly, her voice slamming back at her from empty rooms.

"Mutti! Mutti!" she called with desperation.

At last, she came to a door that resisted her. Inge pushed and pushed against it, until it opened, and she stumbled headlong into a windowless room bright as day, without an obvious light source. White-faced people stood tightly wedged around the walls, staring out of terror-black eyes at a horse's head severed at the neck, suspended by a rope from the center of the ceiling. The head was swinging in slow wide circles, spattering drops of warm blood on the people, like some awful benediction. Each time a drop fell on one of them, he would gasp out a hollow sound, like wind in a tunnel.

"Mutti! Mutti!" Inge screamed, but her voice did not carry.

SPRING INTO WINTER

The faces were all alike--white, with black holes for eyes and mouth, sexless. Every hollow gaze was fixed on the horse's head, whose eyes glowed red.

"Mutti! Mutti!"

Inge groped for the door, but could not find it. She *must* find the door. But there was no door.

A drop of blood splatted thickly on her forehead. Inge screamed and screamed. From the open mouths around her, the wind shrieked and howled.

"Mutti!"

She woke up, sobbing wildly. Her pajamas were soaked with perspiration. Frau Landmann was there in her nightgown, and Doris, and the light was blazing. The old lady cradled the sobbing, shaking child in her arms like a baby.

After a while, Inge quieted down. The night shrank back to normal. Doris brought her fresh pajamas and made her drink a glass of warm milk. She carried her into the master bedroom where Frau Landmann tucked her into her husband's bed. Then she stroked Inge's hair until at last, after a few more tear-stained hiccups, she fell asleep.

From then on, Inge nightly shared her grandmother's room.

- Chapter 12 -

On Monday, November 7, Herschel Grynszpan, a young Polish Jew, in despair about German treatment of his family, shot and fatally wounded a German embassy attaché in Paris. To Jews in Germany, the reaction to this act was the first thunderclap from a threatening sky, soon to explode into a full-fledged storm. They went about their business with drawn faces.

Pale, and looking tired, Frau Landmann said, "We haven't heard the end of this. You mark my words."

At school the next day, the other girls avoided Inge more than usually. Even Irmgard failed to respond to her attempts at conversation, and she was deeply hurt. Wherever Inge went, groups parted in silence. On the streetcar to and from school, people turned away, most of them with glee, some with embarrassment or sadness. The tram conductor on the way home took Inge's money for the fare gingerly, avoiding contact with her hand. He dropped her ticket onto the dirty floor, where she had to retrieve it.

Supper was a silent gathering, that evening. Frau Landmann, Doris and Inge ate without appetite, pushing the food about on their plates. Suddenly, Doris shivered and clutched her hands over her breast. Inge hunched her shoulders and drew her breath in sharply. Frau Landmann let her glasses slip down the bridge of her nose and glared over them at the two girls.

"Come, children." She cleared her throat noisily. "It can't be as bad as all that! Let's clear the table, and then we'll go and have a little glass of wine. You too, Inge."

Inge looked up, surprised. She had never been allowed to taste alcohol, not even the ceremonial wine on holy days. It had become a custom, at times when wine was served, that she take a pretend sip from the foot of the glass, then drank her own "goose wine", a euphemism for water. The situation must be serious, if she was to drink real wine!

The clatter of plate on plate and the metallic tinkle of silverware made reassuring sounds in the brooding house. The Imhoffs, as usual, kept quietly to their own quarters.

The drawing room was lit only by the table lamp, and its little circle of light created a comforting oasis in the chilly gloom. Frau Landmann solemnly poured wine into three glasses. She had brought it up from the cellar while Inge helped Doris with the dishes.

Inge felt magnanimous, positively virtuous, as she dried the plates and cutlery that Doris handed her: she had never before helped with the dishes without being ordered to do so. The tension of waiting--for what, they did not know--was such that any movement, any gesture however trivial, was an affirmation of life.

Frau Landmann filled Inge's glass as full as Doris's and her own. Inge realized that she was admitted--if only on a temporary basis--to the club of adulthood. She held her glass up to the light, turning it slowly this way and that, and admired the liquid ruby sparkle and transparency. Her grandmother leaned over and clinked glas-

Chapter 12

ses with her and Doris.

"Prosit!" the old lady said, "drink up! And may you enjoy many more of this quality." Her deep voice was slightly hoarse.

They drank. Inge sipped a little and knotted her mouth into a tight circle. She wrinkled her nose. The stuff was sour!

Frau Landmann was observing her. She smiled.

"Not to your taste?" she inquired.

Inge swallowed the wine, now diluted with saliva. "Oh yes!" she gasped, "it's delicious!" And to demonstrate her newly-acquired sophistication, she drank again.

Warmth followed the liquid to her stomach, and as she sipped again and again, started to spread outwards. To get the sour stuff down quickly, she tilted the glass and finished the wine with a gulp. Slowly, the warmth pervading her changed to a feeling of velvet. Everything around Inge was velvet, deep red velvet, and soon there were no sharp edges left in the world. She blinked at her grandmother, puzzled by her soft, changing outlines. Trying to improve her vision, she rubbed her eyes with her fists. An uncontrollable grin spread over her face. She leaned back into the corner of the sofa. Dimly, she heard Oma and Doris converse, their voices reaching her through cloudy billows of cotton. Her head was filled with cotton. No, not cotton...it was velvet, deep, red velvet.

"Mmmm..." she sighed, enjoying the wonderful softness that cradled her.

Frau Landmann and Doris looked at her, and nodded to each other. Inge held out her glass at the end of a stiff arm, waving it slightly from side to side.

"More!" she said thickly, "I want more!"

"That's enough, for the first time," Frau Landmann said. "Time for bed now."

She did not want to go to bed. Oma and Doris kept pestering her.

"Up with you. Up you get!"

"Oh all right. All *right*! But it isn't fair! I know you just want to get rid o'me..."

Inge's lower lip trembled, tears formed in her eyes, her nose prickled. Her words were losing their sharp endings--it was humiliating. She tried to get up, but kept falling back.

"Damn!" she said. She was flushed bright red, and her hair seemed fairer than ever in contrast with her face.

Frau Landmann tightened her lips over a laugh.

"I wonder if I did the right thing," she mused aloud.

Doris was watching Inge with disapproval.

"She's drunk," she said.

The old lady shrugged hugely.

"Oh well," she said, "at least she's happy, and warm, and she'll sleep well. Come, help me get her upstairs."

Frau Landmann grasped Inge under one arm, while Doris held her around the middle and led her towards the stairs. Inge muttered indistinctly.

"I'll manage her by myself, Frau Landmann," Doris said. "You go and rest."

Chapter 12

The old lady switched on the hall lights and watched the pair's progress up the stairs. Doris was practically carrying the child.

In bed, after Doris had undressed her and slipped on her pajamas, Inge sank into a cloud of heaving gray. Her bed was afloat on swelling seas, and she held on to the quilt with both hands. Soon she would be asleep, she knew. Then a pinpoint of consciousness pierced her, and for a moment, she was wide awake. She must wait for Oma!

She had wondered if death was contagious. Lying in a dead man's bed left for years undisturbed, Inge had nightly waited with tingling scalp for the chill of death to creep through her own body. In the week that she had shared her grandmother's room, she had been unable to fall asleep until the old lady had joined her, much later. She had pretended sleep, so that she would not have to account for her wakefulness. And while she was lying awake, she had surreptitiously watched her grandmother prepare for bed.

She had watched the old woman strip off one layer after another of her daytime armor, down to the huge creaking corset that encased her from armpit to thigh. Then she would see her slip on a pink quilted robe and disappear in the bathroom, to return without her teeth.

After removing the robe and shaking herself into the tent of her nightdress, Oma would brush her silver-white hair vigorously, then braid it for the night. From the capacious handbag that nightly stood on the marble-topped dresser beside an array of silver-backed brushes, mirror and comb, the old lady fished a small white bowl and an egg. She cracked the shell sharply on the bowl's edge and, dropping the yolk expertly from half-shell to half-shell, she allowed the white to slither into the dish. Frau Landmann lifted the yolk to her mouth, tilting her head, and slurped it with obvious enjoyment, smacking her lips.

Then she dipped three fingers into the eggwhite and slapped the slimy stuff onto her face, working it carefully into the wrinkles around her eyes, into the skin of forehead and cheeks and, with a fresh dip, into the loose folds of skin that drooped from her chin to the top of her chest.

In the morning, the bowl was always gone, and Inge wondered if she had dreamed the whole episode. Only, the next night, the same thing would happen.

Eggs were scarce, Inge was thinking vaguely as her bed lifted her up another swell and then dipped down with her towards heavy sleep. *She* only got one a week, for Sunday breakfast. "Eggs aren't good for children," Oma had said. Oh well.

Someone was roughly shaking Inge's shoulder. She opened slits of eyes and snapped them shut again. The lights were blazing in the room and her grandmother was standing over her. Inge's tongue was furry in her mouth and tasted sour. She shrugged away from the old lady's hand and tried to turn over, shut out the brutal light. But there was no escape.

"Get up! Get up this instant!" Frau Landmann's voice was urgent. "Come on, up! Doris!" she called, "bring me a wet sponge!"

Chapter 12

At the mention of a wet sponge, Inge sat up abruptly. She groaned. Her head spun.

"What... what's the matter?" she asked. "What time is it?"

"Eleven. We have to get *going*!"

Doris appeared with an armful of Inge's clothes, and between the two of them, Frau Landmann and the young girl managed to dress the confused child. Inge noticed vaguely that both her grandmother and Doris were wearing a lot of clothes, and were perspiring.

Frau Landmann cast a quick glance around the bedroom, then switched out the lights. The landing was in darkness, as was the hall below. There was no light anywhere.

Inge stumbled along between the two women, out the front door that Frau Landmann shut softly behind them and then locked, and into the blackness of the night. The damp cold air touched Inge's face with clammy fingers, and she became more alert. A man was waiting by the look-out bench, but Inge was too befuddled still to recognize him. She heard him give swift whispered directions. Then he led her grandmother on by the arm while Doris and Inge followed, holding on to the old lady's clothes.

They climbed into the back of a van parked without lights in the street. The garden gate shut soundlessly behind them. Inside the van, there were benches along the sides, and bars behind the driver's cabin and over the little window in the rear door. The three huddled together closely. Then the van started, and at last Inge was fully awake.

SPRING INTO WINTER

"Where are we going?" she whispered, awed by the others' silence. "Who is that man?"

"Hush." Frau Landmann tucked an arm around Inge and held her tightly. "It's your friend's father, Herr Flasche." She stopped to take a few deep breaths. "He is taking us to jail."

Inge tried to shake herself free. She stiffened.

"To jail!" she exclaimed, indignant. "Why to jail? We haven't done anything!"

"There's going to be trouble tonight. He came to warn us, after you'd gone to bed. He's taking us to jail so we won't get... before we can get hurt."

Through the little barred window in the back, and from the front, beyond the silhouette of their driver, Inge saw a flickering red glow, as though they were driving through a living sunset. "Fire," she thought, but did not say it aloud, "we're driving through fire." She swung around to Doris and heard her sobbing quietly. She fumbled for the older girl's hand and held on to it. Their fingers interlaced, and so linked they sat during the short trip to prison, while the red glow around them changed into black night again. Frau Landmann kept her arm around Inge, and the girls' hands seemed to grow together. They sat in silence.

- Chapter 13 -

Because it was night, and she was tired and still groggy from her heavy sleep, Inge was only dimly aware of entering the prison building. Herr Flasche, wearing his policeman's uniform with the peaked cap, ushered the three to high desks behind which other policemen were enthroned. There, they were registered and Frau Landmann was made to hand over any valuables she carried in her purse.

Then, they were delivered into the care of a female warden who took them up two, three floors in a clanging open-fronted elevator. The building smelled of school, Inge thought, and of public lavatories. It was pervaded by a sour, undefinable stench mixed with carbolic soap. Later, Inge came to recognize the stench as the emanation of hopelessness.

The new prisoners' footsteps along the cement passages made hollow echoes. At dim intervals, naked lightbulbs in wire cages lit their way. The little group stopped at the end of an endless-seeming passage and the warden, a silent woman in starched blue, unlocked the last cell on the right and pushed them in. The gate clanged shut. The passage swallowed up the warden's rubber-soled retreat.

"Well, our home away from home!" Frau Landmann said. She did not bother to lower her voice, and angry shushings came from other cells.

SPRING INTO WINTER

Their new abode was lit by the bulb hanging in the passage outside the door, which consisted of a hinged portion of the metal bars that made up the entire corridor wall. The side walls and the narrow end one were cement; there was no window. Gray tiles covered the floor. Hinged on one wall, secured by two iron-link chains, hung a horizontal board, covered by a thin straw mattress. Beyond this, the cell was bare.

"We may as well get some sleep," Frau Landmann said, lowering herself cautiously on to the pallet. It creaked as she lay down. She pulled her heavy coat over her bulk, kicked off her shoes and turned her head towards Inge and Doris. "Why don't you two spread your coats on the floor, and lie on those," she said. "It won't be too bad, for one night."

The girls did so in silence and presently, chilled and exhausted, they slept.

Morning came with a frenzied ringing of bells. The three new inmates sat up bemused, sore and stiff from the uncomfortable bedding.

Small shuffling groups of women dressed in identical gray entered one after another an open door across the passage and after a while, filed out again, herded back to their cells. A female warden stood guard by the door which, to judge by the pungent odor of carbolic soap and urine issuing from it, gave access to the washroom.

From time to time, the woman on guard barked an order to "Hurry! Hurry!" and the sullen-faced prisoners would temporarily speed up their procession. After the last of them had gone, the warden unlocked Frau Landmann's cell and motioned the three into the washroom.

Chapter 13

Along one wall was a row of open cubicles containing toilets, and facing that, a row of washbasins. A barred window high up near the ceiling admitted a grudging morning light.

The woman stood in the doorway, her arms crossed on her chest, and watched Frau Landmann and the girls at their ablutions. As the old lady removed her dentures to rinse them under running water, the warden walked over, reaching out a red hand.

"No dentures allowed," she said.

Frau Landmann slammed them back into her mouth. "You keep your hands off me!" she roared. "And let me tell you another thing: that... that so-called *bed* I slept on is a scandal! A scandal, I say! I demand a better mattress!"

The warden's mouth opened and snapped shut. She was not used to back-talk from her lodgers. Her arms fell to her side, exposing her huge bust sternly confined by the blue uniform, and prevented from spilling over her stout waist by a leather belt from which dangled a bunch of keys. Her hair was scraped back from her forehead, she wore steel-rimmed pince-nez; her mouth was a colorless slash. She remained speechless; two red spots burned in her cheeks. At last, gasping for composure, she flapped her arms weakly in the direction of the cell and shooed the new jailbirds back into it. Then she slammed the gate on them viciously. The echo receded metallically down the passage.

Presently, a smell of *ersatz* coffee and a sound of clanging announced the arrival of a detail of women with breakfast. From huge enameled pots, they poured malt-

and-chicory with milk into battered tin cups and passed them through the bars of the cells, accompanied by a hunk of coarse black bread.

Frau Landmann refused the beverage after tasting it, but found the bread much to her liking.

"All the goodness of the husk left in it," she said. She chomped happily with clicking dentures. "I am glad to see that my tax money at least feeds people well in our jails!"

After breakfast, the old lady reached into the top of her dress and, to Inge's amazement, withdrew a thick wad of banknotes from between her breasts. She stowed the money in her handbag, that she had refused to give up upon entering the jail, and winked at the two girls.

"Never let yourself be caught empty-handed!" she said.

Since they were not expected to stay, the three were not issued the gray prison garb. Time grew long for Inge. Neither Oma nor Doris seemed much disposed to talk. Soon, she found nothing new to discover by looking through the bars of the cell. She had noticed that besides the washroom across from them, the passage was lined with cells identical to theirs. Snatches of subdued conversation could be heard issuing from them, and once in a while, a shriek or a guffaw. Inge wondered at her grandmother's placidity.

Mid-morning, the warden reappeared with two women prisoners nearly hidden under the bulk of straw mattresses. They threw two of them onto the bunk, and two more onto the floor.

Chapter 13

Frau Landmann asked the warden if there was any news. The woman shrugged, while the two prisoners stood rigidly at attention by the gate, their faces blank.

"Been some looting, and some burning," the warden said grudgingly. "And we got a few more like you in here," she looked the old lady up and down. "Down below, they are."

The two prisoners flicked a glance at each other, then looked straight ahead again.

"All right, you!" the warden told them. "Back to your cells!"

As they turned to leave, when Frau Landmann asked, "Tell me, do you know where... where the burning took place?"

The warden shook her head. "I wasn't there," she said. "Did hear that your synagogue got burned down. And good riddance too, I'd say!" She tossed her head, and the two women in gray snickered briefly.

The three then marched out of the cell, and the gate clanged shut.

"You, there!" Frau Landmann called after them. The warden turned around. "I want you back here, when you've disposed of those two," the old lady continued. Then she added under her breath, so that only the warden could hear it, "You won't regret it."

"Ayeee, ayeee!" Doris was wailing, "the temple burned!"

"Hold your peace, child," Frau Landmann told her. "Your God can take care of himself."

"How can you talk like that? How can you? Ayeee, the temple, burned!"

SPRING INTO WINTER

The old lady shrugged and turned her back on Doris, muttering under her breath something about the lack of self-control of the younger generation. Presently, the warden returned, her eyes sharp with greed. She stepped up close to the cell and stood there, her red hands folded piously. Frau Landmann lifted her handbag onto her lap and opened it with deliberate slowness.

"What's your name?" she asked, crackling the banknotes in the belly of the bag. The warden glanced at it out of the corner of her eye.

"Frau Müller," she said.

The old lady raised her head. Although the other woman towered over her, she managed to look down her nose at Frau Müller. Money changed hands.

"Now then," Frau Landmann said, "I would like you to do me a little favor. First, get me the newspapers. And some books. Children's books, too," she added, glancing at Inge. "Then I want a kilo of grapes, purple ones. Yes. That should do for now. You may go."

Frau Müller, flushed scarlet, gulped. She drew herself up to her full height; her bosom jutted, fit to bust her buttons. She breathed fast through angry nostrils. Then she swung around on her heel and started to walk away. Before she could take a step, Frau Landmann called her back.

"Oh, and Frau Müller," she said blandly, "don't you think you could leave the gate unlocked? We have no intention of escaping, you know, and the child could do with some exercise."

The warden gripped the bars until her knuckles showed white.

Chapter 13

"This is a prison, Ma'am," she managed to get out at last, "not a damn hotel!" She took a few deep breaths and added in a milder tone, "I can't do that, not without permission I can't."

Again Frau Landmann reached into her bag. She thrust her hand through the bars, and Frau Müller accepted the offering.

"See that you get it, then," the old lady said.

"I'll see what can be done, Frau Landmann," the woman said, mollified. "It's not as if you was criminals, is it?" And she marched off down the passage.

"That's the way to handle that kind of person," Frau Landmann said after the warden had disappeared. "She was eating out of my hand! Never let them see you are afraid."

"But Oma," Inge said, "you're not afraid, are you?" Fear was now gripping her own insides.

The old lady glanced at Doris, pursed her lips, and said, "No, Inge, not afraid. Not me. Just a little... just a little *uneasy*, let me put it this way."

Inge was unable to get her grandmother to say more, and Doris was no use at all. She was sitting on a mattress on the floor, hugging her knees and rocking back and forth, moaning softly. Inge was proud of Oma's fortitude, and not a little pleased with her own.

Before long, the requested articles arrived. Frau Landmann gave Doris and Inge each a small cluster of grapes, and some of the books Frau Müller had brought. She herself settled down on the cot with the newspapers.

She read aloud the report of how the people, justly angered by the murderous act of a Jewish criminal against an honored son of the Fatherland, last night had taken revenge into their own hands. A little looting had taken place, nothing serious; a little burning, a few unfortunate deaths--purely accidental--had occurred. But was not the wrath of the people justified? The Jew was sucking the very lifeblood from Mother Germany. It was high time that he were brought to account. And so it went on.

What the paper failed to mention, as Frau Landmann found out later and told the others, was that the looting, the burning and the killing had been carefully orchestrated and ordered from above, and carried out by the Storm Troopers and Hitler's other loyal supporters. The police had been ordered to stand by and not to interfere. The people had in fact taken little active part.

Meanwhile, Frau Landmann, Doris and Inge remained in jail under 'protective' custody. Bruhlefeld was a moderate-sized city, and Frau Landmann had always been one of its most prominent citizens. In the past, she had supported many a local charity and the city, despite the stressful times, did not entirely forget this. The old lady and her young companions were not molested during their sojourn in jail; indeed, they were treated as well as possible under the circumstances. The animosity of individuals was not allowed to get out of hand.

It was however ironic that only wealthy Jews enjoyed the 'protection' of the police, thus leaving their homes and possessions unprotected.

For a while, Inge even enjoyed the novelty of life in prison. It was after all a new experience, and with the curiosity natural to her age, she welcomed any kind of departure from routine.

Chapter 13

After lunch--thick lentil soup with salt pork (even for the Jewish inmates; if they refused it, they had to go meatless) and a chunk of bread--Inge was allowed to explore the passage. While Oma demanded another and yet another serving of soup--"Delicious!" she declared--Inge peered curiously into the other cells.

Gray-faced women sat sullenly on their bunks, or paced about like caged wolves. They stared out resentfully with sunken eyes at the child roaming free. Inge remembered her recent nightmare, and shuddered. Instinctively, her hand reached behind her, groping for a door she knew she would not find. The derisive smile on one woman's face brought her back to reality, and she moved on, blushing. Some women turned away as Inge passed. What had brought them to this place? she wondered.

On the same side as their own cell, halfway along the passage and across from the elevator cage, was a wide window, securely barred. It gave onto the well formed by the four wings of the prison. The window sill was too high for Inge to see the yard below, but she noticed on all sides windows identical to this one: blind, and strongly barred. No escape. Inge returned to her cell, glad of Doris and Oma's familiar companionship.

Later, when the lights in the passage were switched on, Inge asked in a small voice, "When are we going home?"

"I don't know, child, I can't tell," Frau Landmann said. "But I think, tomorrow. Maybe."

"Not another night in this place!" Inge wailed. The novelty had lost its charm. Despite her grandmother's apparent buoyancy, the general ambiance of hostility and despair affected the child, and she wanted out.

"Oh well..." She shrugged resignedly. Protesting would be pointless.

For the first time since their incarceration, it seemed, Doris spoke. "We are lucky, you know," she said. "We are lucky to be here for a little while only. Think of those other poor women..." Her voice trailed off.

In her mind's eye, Inge saw again the hopeless women she had glimpsed as she passed their cells. Some of them were quite young. One face in particular she remembered, a worried white face with horizontal furrows in a high forehead, and vertical ones above the nose. The woman's yellow hair was scraped back, exposing dark roots. She had stared stonily at Inge, her thin mouth pulled down at the corners, and then she had spat on the floor and turned her back. Inge had not resented the gesture, she had merely been curious. How long had that poor woman been there? she had wondered, and how long would she have to stay? And why was she here at all? Perhaps she had a child at home, a little girl?

"I suppose we *are* lucky," Inge agreed, and swallowed.

That night, they slept on the mattresses. It was an improvement on the coats, but not much. Frau Landmann creaked about on the cot above them, the dentures which she had not removed, clicking in her mouth.

The next day was a repetition of the one before. The old lady again bribed Frau Müller to provide them with extras--Frau Landmann was passionately addicted to grapes.

Inge had lost all desire to roam the passage, and lolled dejectedly about in the cell. She riffled through her

Chapter 13

books. Baby books they were, and she was accustomed to meatier reading. For a change, she read them backwards, and got a few laughs that way. She played cat's cradle with Doris, using a length of wool pulled out of her knitted cardigan, to her grandmother's disapproval.

At midday, lentil soup was served again, and Frau Landmann urged Inge and Doris to ask for second helpings, like herself.

"If you don't want them, hand them over!" she said. "I'll finish them."

Inge marveled at Oma's appetite for lentil soup. She must have eaten fully five bowls that time!

As night fell on that second day, Frau Müller came to release them. She escorted them down to the reception desk where Frau Landmann signed papers testifying that they had been treated well and that none of their personal effects were missing. Then they were led to a prison van that stood waiting in the yard and a police driver-- not Herr Flasche this time--drove them home.

The house loomed heavy and sullen out of the night. Only the Imhoffs' lights were burning, high above them, haloed like stars on a misty night. As the van drove off with a roar, Frau Landmann unlocked the front door. Out of the silence, the chill of a dead house struck their faces.

- Chapter 14 -

It was early yet, just after six. Frau Landmann switched on the lights. Inge blinked in the sudden brightness. When her eyes had adjusted to the light, she was surprised that everything seemed unchanged. How could it, after what they had just been through? Yet somehow, there was a subtle shifting of planes, a different dimension. Perhaps it was the rancid air, the utter stillness. It seemed exaggerated after such a short absence. Inge sniffed, uneasy. But all she could determine was an elusive pungency, a memory of a cigarette smoked in the hall, some time ago.

Frau Landmann turned back toward the front door and imperiously rang the Imhoffs' bell.

Doris and Inge were wandering around the hall, touching the walls gingerly, picking up objects and setting them down again, when the tenants came down. Herr and Frau Imhoff were holding hands. Before descending the last flight of stairs, they peered cautiously over the banisters. When they saw Frau Landmann and the girls, they hurried down the last steps.

Herr Imhoff cleared his throat. His wife's eyes were red-rimmed, but it was she who spoke first. Frau Imhoff was a small mousy woman with quick nervous gestures.

"My dear Frau Landmann!" she exclaimed, "I'm so happy to see you home! So very happy! And you too, Inge!" She gave Inge a quick hug.

Chapter 14

Herr Imhoff coughed. "Glad to see you back, ladies. Glad to see you," he said, and hesitated before adding, "Why don't you come upstairs, all of you, and Frau Imhoff will make us a nice cup of coffee. You probably feel thecold." He rubbed his hands together nervously and looked around. "And perhaps it would be better if we turned off the lights, down here. Wouldn't you say so, Maria?"

"Yes, yes indeed," his wife agreed.

Again Herr Imhoff cleared his throat. Perhaps he has caught a cold, Inge thought. She looked at him curiously, but he did not seem ill, just uncomfortable, as though he had some insect crawling inside his shirt. Inge wanted to giggle at the thought, but quickly put a hand over her mouth.

"Not that anything has happened here, you understand," Herr Imhoff told the old lady. "Not... not after the first night, that is..."

Frau Landmann looked sharply at her tenant, but he turned his head away, as did his wife when the old lady looked at her.

What about the looting and the burning? Inge wondered. Nothing seemed to be out of place here, and yet... Somehow, it did not seem right to come home after having spent two days and nights in jail and find things unchanged, just as though nothing had happened.

Frau Landmann, after hesitating briefly, accepted the Imhoffs' invitation. They looked relieved, and grateful. The old lady switched off all but the stair lights, and they trooped upstairs.

On the second floor landing, near the door to the Imhoffs' stairs, a row of suitcases stood lined against the wall. All the other doors were closed.

"What's the meaning...?" Frau Landmann started, but Frau Imhoff quickly took her arm and urged her up the stairs.

"We'll explain," she said, "we'll explain everything. But first, let's go upstairs. Please." She fairly pulled the old lady along.

"That's right," Herr Imhoff added from behind them. "Come on up. We'll explain everything, over a nice cup of coffee."

They entered the steamy little kitchen Inge remembered so well from her Easter and Christmas visits. The scrubbed kitchen table and its four chairs, the shiny brown linoleum floor redolent of polish, the gleaming white gas range and above it, a mantle crowded with kewpie dolls, plaster dwarfs, and family photos in silver frames. Strange, Inge thought, that I know this place so well, yet I see it only twice a year.

Frau Imhoff led the old lady to a rocking chair on the far side of the table and helped her sit down. She placed an upholstered footstool under her feet and arranged some cushions at her back.

"There!" she said with a fleeting smile. "Are you comfortable?"

Before Frau Landmann could answer, their hostess had turned away. Patting kitchen chairs, she invited Doris and Inge to sit down. Then she scuttled over to the range.

Chapter 14

"You must excuse us for receiving you in the kitchen," she said, her back turned. "But we haven't got the stove lit in the living room, and it's a cold night."

The central heating came up only to the second floor, and the Imhoffs as a rule heated their apartment with a coke-burning stove.

"Don't give it a thought, Frau Imhoff, I'm perfectly happy to be here. It's very comfortable. But tell me..."

"Frau Landmann," Herr Imhoff interrupted, "you will forgive me...I know you must be wondering. The suitcases, downstairs..."

He looked beseechingly at the old lady, unable to continue. Frau Landmann nodded.

"It's like this, you see," Herr Imhoff went on with an effort. He stared down at his slippered feet and twisted his hands. "You see, we...The fact is, we have to leave."

Frau Landmann's lips worked silently. Inge stared at her in fascination. A sound of clattering came from the range where Frau Imhoff clumsily shifted the coffee pot and cups around.

"After all this time...," Frau Landmann said at last, softly. "How long has it been, Herr Imhoff? How many years?"

"Frau Landmann, don't! How many years? We've been your only tenants. We'd just got married...Maria?"

His wife turned towards them a face now suffused with weeping. "Fifteen years, Karl. We've been married...fifteen years. Ohhh!" She burst into sobs and ran to the old lady, threw her arms around her neck. Frau Landmann patted her shoulder absently.

"There, there," she said, as one would soothe a child. Her own eyes remained dry and stared fixedly over the younger woman's prematurely graying head. At last, she pushed her away gently and, setting her hands on the arms of the rocking chair, levered herself up.

"Come, children," she said to the silent girls. "We'd best go down. These poor people must have a lot to attend to."

She looked slowly around the comfortable kitchen, then, her feet dragging a little, she moved towards the door. Inge and Doris followed. What about the coffee? Inge thought. She had never had coffee before, except at the prison, and that was ersatz. She wanted to taste real coffee. But then, she thought, the Imhoffs probably drank ersatz, anyway. After all, they weren't rich.

Herr Imhoff had jumped up and, holding his sobbing wife in his arms, tried to detain them.

"Your coffee!" he said. "Frau Landmann, your coffee!"

By the door, the old lady turned around. "Never mind, now, Herr Imhoff. Another time..." Then, realizing that there would be no other time, she smiled a little sadly. "Herr Imhoff, we've always been good friends. I know we are parting good friends." She paused, searching for words. "I know that you are leaving because we...because you...I know that you *have* to leave. That's the way things are, these days. Believe me, I don't think any the less of you. Good night."

She turned back to the room and held out her hand. Herr Imhoff let go of his wife, and took it in both of his. He pumped it up and down as though he would never

Chapter 14

release it. Then the old lady kissed Frau Imhoff gently. Doris and Inge waited by the door. Inge's mouth was dry.

As they started down the stairs, Herr Imhoff ran after them, his slippers slapping on the steps.

"Here!" he said, thrusting a white paper bag into Inge's hand, "it's for you!"

Inge opened it. Sugar eggs! And in November! She smiled up at Herr Imhoff, but he had already vanished into the kitchen.

Back on the second floor, Frau Landmann furiously switched on one light after another.

"What the hell!" she shouted, "let them know we are home! Let them come if they want!"

"Oma! Oma!" Inge tried to restrain her. "You mustn't! We shouldn't!"

"Let go of me, child!" Frau Landmann roared, shaking off Inge's hands. "I want lights! Lights!"

Tears running unchecked down her cheeks, she continued switching on the light in room after room.

Doris pulled Inge into her room, the one that had been Grete's. Years and years ago, it seemed. At first, she stood rigidly in the middle of the room, then flung herself sobbing into Doris's arms. She wept with rage, with pity for her grandmother and yes, with compassion for Doris. In the back of her consciousness, premonition grew of the coming end of life as she knew it.

For a long time, Doris said nothing. It seemed as though, over the last few weeks, she had almost lost the power of speech. She rocked Inge silently, awkwardly, then pulled a handkerchief from her pocket and wiped the child's tears.

"Come," she said, "we should not leave your grandmother alone."

Inge gulped to regain her self-control. By now, Oma was probably in her own room, she thought. She freed herself gently from Doris's arms and crossed the passage to the room she shared with Oma. The door was still closed.

Inge heard her grandmother still charging around downstairs, turning on one light switch after another until the house was ablaze with light, as it had not been for years. Inge opened the bedroom door and turned on the wall switch. What she saw made her gasp.

"Oma...," she whispered, as she took in the state of the room. Then she shrieked, "Oma! Oma!"

Doris appeared at her shoulder, and she, too, gasped.

"Oh, my God!" she whispered.

Wrecked furniture, broken glass littered the room. The white built-in wardrobes were splintered from top to bottom, as though a maniac had taken an ax to them. The clothes they had contained were strewn about the floor, ripped apart. The quilts, the pillows and mattresses of the beds had been disemboweled and their contents spilled about in feathery disarray. It was more an abandoned battlefield, than a room.

Inge felt sick, her ears were singing with a high-pitched whine. She did not notice Oma's presence until she was roughly pushed aside. The old lady looked wild, her cheeks streaked with tears, her hair falling in thin strands over forehead and ears. She was breathing in great snorting gulps.

Chapter 14

Frau Landmann assessed the damage at a glance, then strode directly to the middle wardrobe, peering into the splintered mess. She placed her hands on her hips; her chest was heaving.

"Curious, isn't it," she said calmly--too calmly. "Curious, that this should be the only room they touched." She turned to Inge. "Have *you* any idea why?"

Inge shook her head dumbly and swallowed against the dryness in her throat. Frau Landmann pointed a shaking finger at the wardrobe.

"Notice what's missing?"

Again Inge shook her head. Her mouth filled with bitter saliva.

"The safe! The safe's been looted!" the old woman roared.

Inge backed away, bumped into Doris behind her.

"And who would know where to find the safe?" Frau Landmann went on relentlessly.

Inge's mouth fell open. "I don't know," she croaked, "*I* didn't know where..." She clapped her hand to her mouth and her eyes grew huge.

She pushed past Doris and ran headlong to her own room. The bed had not been slept in since she had shared her grandmother's room. But Inge still kept her belongings there, and the doll Amalia lived enthroned on the cushion Grete had given her on her birthday.

Now Amalia lay in the middle of the quilt, her head smashed, her porcelain arms wrenched out at the shoulders. Inge stared down at her for what seemed a lifetime. No longer was Amalia a symbol for the continuity of life. She was a thing, a poor broken, befouled object. With dragging steps, Inge returned to Frau Landmann's room.

The old lady had pushed a way through the debris and was feverishly searching through the ruins of the safe, which had been built into the back panel of the middle wardrobe. She discarded armfuls of documents, searching, searching for something she could not find. At last, her hands dropped to her sides and she sat down defeated, heavily, at the edge of her gutted bed.

"Just as I thought," she said tonelessly. "*Just* as I thought."

Inge cowered against Doris. She was biting the nail of her forefinger. "Is it... is it the platinum?" she whispered. She felt cold. Nodding in answer to her own question, she said, "Yes, of course it's the platinum. I know who took it."

Frau Landmann regarded her sadly. "You have been showing off," she stated. "Elfriede?"

"Elfriede," Inge whispered. She looked up, her cheeks suddenly flaming, and added loudly, "But Elfriede couldn't have.... She *couldn't* have done this!"

The old lady passed a shaking hand down her face.

"No, of course she couldn't have," she agreed. Her hand fell back into her lap. "But tell me this: what about her brother? Eh? What about that precious no-good brother of hers?"

Inge clenched her teeth until her jaws ached, and shook her fists. "I'll get her," she snarled, "the dirty sneaky thief, you just wait till I get my hands on her!"

Frau Landmann shook her head. "Leave be, child," she said. "Leave Elfriede be. She doesn't know a thing about this, I'll bet."

Chapter 14

"Oh she doesn't, does she! Well, she does, too! Her brother smashed my doll, my beautiful doll! I'll bet he told her, too!" Inge stomped her foot in rage and despair, choking back tears.

Frau Landmann sighed. "Never mind about the doll, now. It's a pity, to be sure," she said. "What's worse, is the loss of your little fortune. That is gone, and gone for good."

"Couldn't we report it to the... to the police?"

Frau Landmann laughed. "You haven't learned yet, have you? We're Jews, remember? Oh, what's the use...." She shrugged, and mechanically started to clear up the mess.

"Come on, you two, give me a hand." The old lady held up an emptied pillow by a corner and dropped it again. "It's illegal, you know, to own that amount of platinum in the first place," she said to Inge. "That boy knew what he was doing, all right."

- Chapter 15 -

Inge did not go back to school next day. What would happen after the week-end, remained to be decided.

The Imhoffs had tried to leave the house quietly, unnoticed, early in the morning, carrying only their suitcases. But Frau Landmann intercepted them. She had been watching out for them.

"Did you know anything about *that*?" she asked, jerking her chin in the direction of her room.

Herr Imhoff stared at his shoes in an agony of embarrassment, and nodded.

"I don't believe for one moment that you or your wife had anything to do with this. I know you didn't," the old lady said. "But since you knew about it, last night, why didn't you tell me? Why didn't you warn me?"

"I couldn't, Frau Landmann," the man said. "I did not dare! They said that if I told on them, they'd come after us!"

Frau Imhoff was clinging to her husband's arm. She looked around as though afraid they might be overheard even now. She was buttoned into a brown winter coat, and its fuzzy fur collar nearly swallowed up her little face, making her appear more mouselike than ever.

"He's right," she said, her voice quavering. "Karl is right. We couldn't tell, honestly we couldn't. They came that night, the night you left for... for...."

"The night we left for jail. Yes."

Chapter 15

Frau Imhoff nodded dumbly.

"We can tell you this much," Herr Imhoff said, clearing his throat. "They rang your bell about midnight. At first, we took no notice. After all," he spread his hands, palms up, "we had no way of knowing that you had gone! Then they started pounding on the door, and ringing our bell as well, and when no one else went to open, I thought I had better go and have a look." He took a shuddering breath. "There were two of them," he went on. "And they made me swear not to tell. Especially not to the police...." Herr Imhoff gazed at the old lady with a puzzled look. "They seemed to know just where to go."

Inge was leaning against Frau Landmann's side, and the old lady laid a shaking hand on her shoulder. "You won't be breaking your promise," she said, "if you will just answer my questions." She waited a moment. Herr and Frau Imhoff looked at each other, then at Frau Landmann. They did not reply, but their eyes were black with fear in their white faces.

"Tell me," Frau Landmann went on firmly, "these men, were they in uniform?"

Herr Imhoff nodded.

"Blue uniform?"

Herr Imhoff shook his head. He was starting to perspire; Inge could see little beads of moisture forming on his upper lip, on his forehead.

"Brown, then?"

Herr Imhoff looked around quickly, then nodded.

"Just as I thought. And now, I won't keep you any longer." Frau Landmann reached out with her free hand and touched Frau Imhoff fleetingly on the cheek. "Good bye, and good luck."

Leaning on Inge for support on one side and her cane on the other, the old lady stepped back into the hall. The front door shut on the Imhoffs. Frau Landmann sighed.

"The end of a chapter," she said. "The end of a chapter...." Then, more briskly, "Come, children, we have work to do."

They returned to the bedroom and resumed the attempt to restore some sort of order in the wreckage. After some time, they were interrupted by the door bell's shrill ringing, and pounding on the door. Frau Grünberg and Hannelore had come on an unannounced visit.

Frau Grünberg seemed to have melted since their last meeting. It was as though only a flaccid shell was left of her former self. Her hair was disheveled, her eyes bloodshot yet dry; her breath was choppy and irregular. Hannelore was a cowering near her grandmother, clinging to her skirt; dried saliva caked the corners of her mouth.

"Oh my baby, my little girl," Frau Grünberg wailed. "My child, my child!" She repeated this over and over, in a sobbing monotone. She clutched Frau Landmann's arm and shaking it, looked up beseechingly into her old friend's face. "My child, my little girl..."

Frau Landmann led the distraught woman to the drawing room, made her sit down in her own deep chair. Hannelore never left her grandmother's side. She clung to the stuff of her skirt as though her fingers had become part of it, as though it was the last support that kept her afloat on an ocean of grief and bewilderment.

Chapter 15

"Drink this," Frau Landmann said, holding a glass of wine to Frau Grünberg's lips. But the old woman shook her head, and at last, tears started to fall. They oozed out of her eyes in milky, searing beads, following a bed of new furrows down the once plump cheeks.

"My daughter, my daughter!" she sobbed.

Frau Landmann had painfully knelt in front of her old friend and was forcing the wine to her lips.

"Drink this at once!" she commanded.

Frau Grünberg drank, choked and sputtered, then obediently drank again. She drained the glass, and gradually a little color returned to her cheeks. Frau Landmann poured a little wine into the glass for Hannelore, and sent Inge for some water to dilute it.

But Hannelore refused to drink. She pressed her lips together and turned her head away. Frau Landmann ordered Inge to take care of the girl and leave the two women to themselves.

Curious, Inge took Hannelore's hand in her own. It was icy to the touch and did not respond to the pressure of her fingers. But she followed Inge without resistance, walking like a jointed doll. Inge tried some small talk, but made no dent in the glazed surface of Hannelore's silence. They went into Inge's old room, where she pushed Hannelore down into her child-sized armchair. She busied herself with her belongings, pulling out drawers and shutting them with a bang, hauling out dresses and hanging them up again. Meanwhile she kept up a continuous chatter, glancing furtively at Hannelore from time to time.

SPRING INTO WINTER

She told about her stay in prison, how well they had been treated, and how much she had enjoyed the sojourn. She knew that Hannelore had not been jailed: surely they would have seen each other.

But like Frau Grünberg, the girl in the armchair seemed to be only a husk: hunched forward, hands upturned in her lap, eyes glazed with a dull film--the real Hannelore was not there. Nor did she react when Inge asked bluntly, "What *has* happened to your mother?"

Something terrible must have occurred, Inge sensed. But if this strange Hannelore did not want to be friends... Inge shrugged. She threw herself onto her bed with her shoes on and pretended to read, until Doris, pale and with feverish eyes, came for Hannelore, to go home with her grandmother.

The girl rose obediently and went along stiffly. She had not uttered a single word the entire time she had been with Inge.

Inge was burning with curiosity. As soon as the front door had closed on the visitors, she slid down the banisters, landing neatly by the drawing room door. Her grandmother was pacing the room with long strides, her cane discarded. She was wringing her hands and looked as wild as the night before. She refused to answer Inge's questions.

"Go away, child, leave me alone. Leave me be," she said in a strangled voice quite unlike her usual boom.

It was not until years later, in fact, that Inge learned what had happened to Hannelore's parents. By then, Hannelore herself had perished in a concentration camp, and Inge was sorry that she had not been kinder to her

Chapter 15

when she had had the chance.

It had been about ten o'clock the previous night that the telephone rang in the dentist's home and a man at the other end asked for him. The dentist took the receiver from his wife.

"Please, doctor, you must help me! I'm in agony!" said a whining man's voice.

"Who is this? Are you one of my patients?"

"No, doctor, I am not. But I can't find anyone to help me, not at this hour!"

"Are you Jewish?"

"No. But I... I..."

"Do you realize that I am allowed to treat only Jewish patients?"

"I know that, doctor, but--oh! oh! I won't tell on you! Just help me, please! I can't stand the pain."

"Have you tried the hospital?"

"It's too far, I have no way of getting there. And your office is just around the corner. Oh, the pain!"

The dentist put his hand over the receiver and looked inquiringly at his wife who stood beside him. She shrugged, pulling down her mouth and putting out her hands with a gesture of helplessness. Frau Grünberg, sitting by the sideboard with her ear near the radio, shook her head vehemently.

"If he's a goy, don't take him, Ernst! Don't take him, not if he's a goy!" She nodded at the radio. "There's more trouble. Don't take him."

The dentist spoke into the receiver. "Are you there? I am sorry, but I cannot take the risk..."

"Doctor! Your oath, your doctor's oath! Remember your doctor's oath! I am in agony, I really am. It's a boil, just needs lancing. I'm sure it's a boil, and I live just around the corner..."

The dentist sighed deeply. "All right, all right, I'll see you. On your own responsibility, mind. And what's your name?"

A note of triumph crept into the voice at the other end. The dentist frowned, puzzled.

"Thank you, doctor," the man said without giving his name. "I'll be right over." And he hung up.

The dentist and his family lived in the apartment above the dental clinic, which occupied the first floor of the building. It would only take a moment to go down.

Frau Grünberg clung to her son-in-law's sleeve, entreating him not to go.

"No good will come of this, I feel it in my bones!" Turning to her daughter, she implored, "You tell him! Don't let him go, don't go with him!" Tears streamed down the old woman's face.

"Control yourself, Mother," the dentist's wife said. "If Ernst feels he must go, he will go. It's his duty as a doctor."

She was her husband's assistant. She removed her slippers and put on the rubber-soled shoes that stood under the clothes rack in the lobby. Frau Grünberg stood hugging herself by the front door, rocking back and forth. Her daughter kissed her as she went out after her husband.

"Take care of Hanne," she said as she left.

Chapter 15

As the dentist reached out to switch on the lights in his office, he was seized from behind. Someone else turned the switch. Someone slammed a hand over his mouth, and yet another had grabbed his wife from behind, clamping her mouth shut too. The double doors-- the inner one leather-padded--were closed and locked. There were six Storm Troopers in the office. Big, sturdy fellows.

"So, doctor," one of them said smoothly to the terrified dentist, "you would lay your filthy Jewish paws on an Aryan, would you?"

He was a blond man, red-faced, and he was leaning back in the swivel chair by the desk, one booted leg crossed over the other, foot swinging. The dentist tried to free himself, but the two men holding him twisted his arms.

"Treat an Aryan, you would, eh? More likely *kill* him, you Jewish swine!" The man rose and swaggered up to the dentist. Deliberately, he kicked him in the shins. The dentist's eyed watered and his glasses steamed up.

The blond man, obviously the leader of the gang, flicked the spectacles off the dentist's nose with a pinkie. They fell onto the carpet without breaking. The man ground his heel into them.

"You won't need these again," he said and grinned, exposing gold-capped incisors.

The woman was struggling against her hold, trying to free herself, to come to her husband's aid.

"Hold her more tightly!" the blond man barked at the two guarding her. "And make sure she watches!"

The sixth man in the meantime had readied the dentist's chair in a reclining position. The two holding the dentist marched him up to it, thrust him into it, and brought out strong ropes with which they tied him down securely. They tied his wrists to the armrests, his feet and legs to the footboard. They twisted the rope around his chest and shoulders and around the back of the chair. The dentist struggled in vain. He tried to shout. One man smacked him across the mouth.

"Shut up, you!" he snarled.

The blond man slipped on the dentist's long white coat that hung on a stand in a corner. It was too small for him, as the dentist was short and stubby. The Storm Trooper flexed his shoulders, and the seams of the coat cracked.

"Never mind," he said, rubbing his hands, "he won't need this again, either." He guffawed. The other men laughed too. The dentist's eyes were bulging, and his wife was weeping silently onto the hand still clapped over her mouth.

The blond man kicked in the glass front of the instrument cabinet and chose a pair of gleaming steel tongs.

"Ready?" he asked his assistants.

They nodded, and one of them licked his lips.

The two who had tied up the dentist, forced his jaws open. The leader rolled up his sleeves; golden hairs glinted on his wrists. He started extracting the dentist's teeth, throwing them onto the floor as they came cracking out. He pushed his knee into his victim's groin to get a better grip. The dentist screamed, gurgling through the blood that was filling his mouth. His wife fainted.

Chapter 15

One of the men holding her slapped her face till she regained consciousness.

Then the blond man pulled down the electric drill and drilled into the sockets left by the extracted teeth. By then, the dentist too had fainted. Blood streaked his balding head, and ran down his chin, soaking his shirt and suit. The Storm Trooper drilled into the roof of the mouth and through the cheeks from the inside. He drilled wherever there was flesh or bone left to drill. The dentist had already choked to death on his own blood. His face, what could be seen of it, had turned blue. But the blond man could not stop drilling. Beads of sweat stood thickly on his forehead, saliva drooled from his mouth. He had lost control over the hand that held the drill. He drilled at last into the dead staring eyes.

Then he told the men who held the dentist's wife to release her. She slumped onto the floor, unconscious.

The leader of the Storm Troopers went to the washbasin and meticulously scrubbed his hands, using the nail brush to remove every trace of blood from under his spatulate fingernails. He shrugged off the stained coat and kicked it into the pool of blood around the dentist's chair, where it slowly started to soak up the viscous red liquid. He wiped his feet on the short Turkish rug near the desk.

"We're through here. Let's go," he said to his helpers after casting a last look around the office.

"What about her?" one of the others asked, pointing his chin at the woman on the floor.

"Leave her be. She'll enjoy herself when she comes to." The man switched off the lights and closed the doors after the men.

SPRING INTO WINTER

When the dentist's wife regained consciousness, she saw the state of things by the street light that crept in stripes through the slits of the venetian blinds. On hands and knees she dragged herself around the dentist's chair, to the instrument cabinet.

"What's the use," she muttered softly, "what's the use."

She clawed her way up to the instruments she knew so well, trying to avoid the jagged splinters of glass. She laughed, once. She groped for a scalpel and slashed her wrists. The right one took longer, as she was not much good with her left hand which by now was slippery with gushing blood. Then she crawled back to her husband and slowly hoisted herself up to him. She lay down on his body, her face on his, and there, after some time, she died.

When her daughter and son-in-law had not returned by two o'clock in the morning, Frau Grünberg crept down the stairs to the office. The Storm Troopers had not relocked the door.

- *Chapter 16* -

The only thing that Inge found out at that time, was that Hannelore's father had been murdered, and that her mother had committed suicide. It was Doris who told her, awed and white-faced.

That day, Inge added a new word to her vocabulary, suicide--*Selbstmord* in German, self-murder--and at the same time learned its meaning. Because it was not only Hannelore's mother who had committed suicide: all over Germany, people died by their own hand. They committed suicide in Berlin, in Düsseldorf and Frankfurt. It was an act committed by friends, relatives and strangers. People jumped from high windows in Breslau or Munich, put their heads in gas ovens in Nuremberg and Bremen, or took overdoses of sleeping pills. In Hamburg or Essen, others slashed their wrists and bled to death in warm baths. Men threw themselves under speeding trains in Bonn and Hanover. All over Germany, Jews were dying. Some took their own lives to avoid a worse death, or to put an end to an existence grown pointless and intolerable. Some, to blot out the vision of loved ones murdered, or the defilement of wives and daughters, of sisters and mothers. All over Germany, Jews realized at last that Hitler had come to stay.

Frau Landmann tried to persuade her old friend to stay with them for the time being. But Frau Grünberg refused. No one else was allowed to do what had to be

SPRING INTO WINTER

done. At least let the child stay, Frau Landmann urged. No, the child also had to come. She must face the realities of death sooner or later. But like this? Frau Landmann had insisted, and at her age? Yes, like this. This was their country, and their life, and their death. They had left.

Up to then, the situation in Germany had been at times unpleasant for Inge, yet in a strange way, exciting. She had actually experienced little personal suffering, and what happened in other places and to people unknown to her, did not affect her own existence. Her grandmother's often-voiced opinion that things would soon return to normal, that this madness could not last, had laid a solid foundation of trust in Inge's life. But the events in Hannelore's home--a girl no older than she!--shocked her into a sudden realization that here, now, was true danger. The madness did *not* go away, it had taken root even in their own quiet hometown. There was no safety anymore.

For those Jewish citizens who, on that Sabbath, might have had the courage to worship openly, there was nowhere to go: the synagogue was a pile of smoldering rubble. All over Germany, a land proud of its enlightenment, its advanced civilization, synagogues were lying in smoking ruins. As time passed, a curious fact emerged: only those temples had been destroyed that did not by their burning or destruction endanger adjoining Aryan property. And many of the Jews who had been taken into "protective custody," had been sent on to concentration camps.

Chapter 16

The next few days were lonely ones, and cold. Jewish children were banned from German schools for good, and Inge rejoiced at the unexpected vacation. A tacit aura of shame hung over the town after Friday night's murder, and the Jews, though now unmolested, kept to their homes as much as possible. They left them only to pay each other furtive visits, and made only the most indispensable purchases from merchants who served them in sullen silence. Rumors grew wildly about more reprisals in retaliation for the Paris assassination.

On Tuesday, a letter arrived from Brussels. Mail was censored, and everything had to be put in equivocal yet innocent words.

"We are appalled at what happened in Paris," Frau Richter wrote. "We are doing our best not to aggravate the situation." How? Inge wondered. "Unfortunately, I am still immobilized with the plaster cast on my leg. We hope to hear from you as soon as possible."

The letter shook in Frau Landmann's hand. "What that means, I suppose, if I understand your mother correctly, is that she won't be able to come here," she said. "It would indeed be foolish for her to try, at this point. Oh well, I will have to take steps from this end. I think we should not waste time."

"What steps, Oma?"

"Why, for your departure, of course!" The old lady seemed surprised that Inge could have forgotten about it.

"Now, Oma? I couldn't leave you now!" A new sense of responsibility, of protectiveness, had been growing in Inge since the wrecking of the bedroom; she felt that, to a great extent, she was guilty.

SPRING INTO WINTER

Frau Landmann smiled fleetingly at the child, and pinched her cheek.

"We had better set your parents' mind at rest straight away," she said, ignoring the last exclamation. "They are worried. Either they did not get my letter, or it crossed theirs *en route*. In any case, it won't hurt to reassure them."

She shuffled over to her desk, leaning heavily on her cane. Inge watched her, uneasiness and pity in her heart.

How slow Oma had become. She used to move with such speed and vigor for a woman of her size. Was this what Oma meant, when she said that she was getting old? Old people die, Inge thought abruptly. Oma must not die! She could not really be old, not her very own, her darling....She fought against a sudden tightness in her throat, took a deep breath, and her eyes filled with tears. Furiously she dashed them away, sniffed, and wiped her nose on the back of her hand. She ran out of the room, to the kitchen, looking for Doris. But Doris was not there.

I have to see *someone*, speak to somebody, Inge thought. She raced up the stairs taking the steps two at a time, and arrived flushed and panting on the landing. The door to Doris's room stood open, and Inge walked in without knocking.

Doris was bent over a suitcase open on the unmade bed. Her clothes were scattered about. Startled, she turned around. The two girls stared at each other in silence. Then, pointing at the suitcase, Inge asked, "What are you doing?"

Chapter 16

Blushing, Doris stood up straight. "Didn't your grandmother tell you?"

"Tell me what?"

"That I have to leave. I'm going home."

"But you can't! You can't leave us here all alone!"

Doris sat on the edge of the bed and patted a place beside her. "Come and sit down," she said.

Inge joined her, but kept her distance. Doris reached out and took the child's hand in her own. She stared down at it intently as though trying to read it, or to avoid meeting Inge's accusing eyes.

"And the fine? Did she tell you about the fine?"

"What fine?" Inge was at a loss.

Doris sighed, and dropped the other's hand. "It really isn't my place to tell you....I do wish your grandmother had told you."

Inge was more and more mystified. Her face begged for enlightenment.

"It's in reprisal, you see," Doris said at last. "For the murder in Paris. The Jewish community has to pay the German government one billion marks in compensation."

Inge was unable to grasp this. One billion marks? It did not mean a thing to her. Ten marks she could understand, or even a million. But one *billion*! That was a fun figure, children used it, it did not exist, not *really*! She laughed.

"That's silly," she said. "One billion isn't a real number."

"Oh yes it is, *and* we'll have to come up with it, all of us, every *pfennig* of it! *And* we're supposed to build up again by ourselves everything *they* destroyed, the other

173

night!"

Inge was still puzzling over the amount of money and ignored the rest of Doris's statements. Ten pfennigs bought quite a decent amount of licorice, she mused, and there were a hundred pfennigs in one mark, so that would make how much licorice? Mountains, glorious black mountain ranges of it! She drew in her breath in awe.

"How much is one billion marks?" she asked then, "and if it's really real, how can we pay it? Do we have that much?"

"We'll all have to cut down on *something*, to help. Your grandmother has to do without me."

Doris turned to Inge, holding out her hands in a gesture of appeal. "I would have stayed on even without pay," she said. "You must believe me! But your Oma won't let me. She said... she said I'd better be with my parents, now. Besides, she'll have to sell the house, and there won't be so much work..."

Inge stiffened. "What do you mean, she has to sell the house? She didn't tell *me*!"

"It's another edict. She...she may have forgotten to tell you. With so *much* on her mind, you understand..."

"She couldn't have forgotten! Not Oma! I know: she's *afraid*, that why she didn't tell me."

It all fell into place now, her grandmother's slow gait, the silences, the caresses begun and never finished. Oma did not have the courage to tell her because she knew how much Inge loved the house. She stood up, pushing her fists deep into her sweater pockets. She paced back and forth in silence, while Doris watched. At last, Inge gave one of the bedposts a violent kick, then hopped

Chapter 16

about on one foot, wincing, while she nursed the other one in her hands.

Now her tears really started to flow, and she abandoned herself to an orgy of sobbing. Yet, strangely, she enjoyed her own pain and misery. She saw herself as from the outside, saw a girl bawling with a square mouth, her nose running, her face red and distorted, the fair hair appearing white by contrast. She also saw Doris waiting helplessly for the storm to pass.

On and on Inge wept, examining the picture of Inge weeping. How ugly! she thought, I never knew how ugly I am! This gave her a new reason for despair, and she went into another paroxysm. Before her eyes passed the images of Hannelore, her dead parents and her grandmother, and she cried for pity. She thought of her own parents who had abandoned her to her fate, while they selfishly lived a life of ease in a friendly country. She cried for hate and frustration. She would *not* go to Belgium to join her heartless parents!

By now, Doris had had her fill of Inge's outburst. She grabbed her by the shoulders and shook her. Inge had not expected this, and the surprise stopped her short. She glared at Doris out of swollen red eyes.

"Traitor! Coward!" she hissed.

Doris shrugged, compressed her lips, and shoved Inge towards the door. "Go away, I have my packing to finish," she said, closed the door on Inge, and locked it. From the other side, Inge gave it a parting kick.

Inge could hear her grandmother's labored typing through the closed drawing room door. Tap, tap, tap-tap.

She went in and slammed the door.

Frau Landmann, turning, looked at her over her glasses, thick fingers still poised over the keys. Hands in pockets, Inge strode over to the old lady.

"Why didn't you tell me that Doris was leaving?" she demanded. "And why didn't you tell me that you were selling the house?"

Frau Landmann sighed. Automatically, she said, "Take your hands out of your pockets."

Just as automatically, Inge did so.

The old lady twisted her own veined hands in her lap. "These are matters for grown-ups," she said.

"Do you take me for a child?"

Frau Landmann looked in silence at the thin ten-year-old, and Inge gazed steadily back at her. She seemed to have grown, not so much in stature, as in understanding and intuition.

"No," Frau Landmann said, "I suppose you aren't the child you used to be." She smiled bitterly. "You have earned your bit of adulthood... and I wish it were not so. I've tried... By God, I have tried."

"Grandmother."

Inge laid her arms around the old woman's neck and kissed the parchment cheek. It was the first time that she had not used the familiar, cozy "Oma." She cradled the white head against her shoulder and stroked the thin hair. Frau Landmann encircled Inge's thin body with her arms and they remained so, eyes at a level, the girl standing near her seated grandmother. Into Inge's nostrils rose the sweet-sour odor of old age, of ultimate decay. Her chest ached with the sadness of it. She was ready to

Chapter 16

give her soul, her very life, to keep Oma with her, always, and she knew that it was not possible, that soon they would have to part.

Doris left, and after her departure, Inge was again obliged to trek down the hill to the village, to shop for groceries.

She made a point of hurrying past the Flasches' house, for fear of seeing Elfriede's pale face grinning at her from behind the lace curtains.

The attitude of the shopkeepers had changed. They spoke barely at all and made Inge feel that they did her a favor by accepting Jewish money in exchange for the poorest quality goods. Even Herr Fritsche, the butcher, only had courage to wink at her, when no one was about.

Frau Landmann's and Inge's needs were small, since the old lady had drastically retrenched their expenses. No fire at all was lit in the house, and the chill pervaded their very bones. Frau Landmann seemed to shrink within her skin, which now hung in loose folds on her face and hands. The coats and dresses she wore unfashionably long anyway, now nearly swept the ground.

After the wrecking of her bedroom, the old lady and Inge slept in the guest room. It also had twin beds. The library was next door, which suited Inge well, since she could easily slip in there when she was unable to sleep. Frau Landmann slept with desperate exhaustion, or perhaps pretended sleep. At any rate, she raised no objections when, at dead of night, Inge rose, wrapped herself in sweaters and stealthily left the room.

SPRING INTO WINTER

After the murder of Hannelore's father, Inge had had another nightmare. She had dreamed that she walked down the village street on garbage collecting day. The full cans stood waiting at the curb. Over the one in front of the butcher's shop, a human body was draped, face down. The body was completely skinned and looked like one of the anatomical charts which Inge had avidly studied in an encyclopedia. The exposed muscles were deep red, touched with blue, with streaks of yellow fat and white sinews. In the dream, it was a hot day in summer, and flies clustered in buzzing clumps, crawling lecherously over the corpse.

Inge woke up drenched in perspiration, retching and shaking. Leaning on one elbow, she peered at the huge dark shape of her grandmother in the other bed. The old lady was breathing in snorting gasps, but did not otherwise stir.

Quietly, Inge crept to the library. She was shivering in her clammy pajamas. She felt that if she could only check on the accuracy of her dream picture, she might banish the ghastly thought. Curiously, her recollection had been faithful in every detail, all but the flies. Inge returned to bed. She clamped her teeth and stared at the ceiling, waiting for the exorcism to work, and did not know when she fell asleep.

And then, assessors poured through the house, little men who kept their hats on and who, after licking their pencils, took notes in little hardcover notebooks. They stalked from room to room, appraising the furniture with mouths pulled down at the corners. They went through

Chapter 16

the house with pinched noses, as though it stank. Inge followed them like a shadow.

"Go away, child," they told her, "stop bothering us. We won't take any of your Jewish things, if that's what is worrying you."

Inge blushed hotly and left them alone.

They set the value of the large house at a mere fraction of its worth. Frau Landmann tried to protest.

The assessors sneered.

"Don't forget that any German who buys your house will be making a sacrifice to the Aryan ideal," they told her. "He will do you a favor, buying it at *any* price. And it will have to be fumigated."

Frau Landmann said nothing. She thrust her cane onto the floor and showed the assessors out.

- Chapter 17 -

Shortly thereafter, a poorly-dressed woman accompanied by a girl of Inge's age came to see Frau Landmann. Surely not a buyer already, Inge thought; she looks too poor, anyway!

Inge tried to start a conversation with the girl, but she clung timidly to her mother's side. She seemed terrified. Frau Landmann shooed Inge out of the room.

"Who were they?" Inge asked at lunch. She had not seen the visitors leave.

"Some poor Jews. *Schnorrers*--beggars."

"Do you know them?"

Frau Landmann turned away and spread margarine thinly on her bread. "They are relations of your grandfather's--may he rest in peace," she said.

"Why didn't you let me talk to the girl, then? She was about my age."

"They weren't staying. What was the point?"

"Why did they come? I've never seen them before. I didn't even know that we had relatives like... that!"

The old lady sighed and looked uneasily at Inge.

"First of all," she said, "they don't live around here. They come from a village in Westphalia. And then, we never knew them...socially. Don't jump on your high horse, miss!" she added hastily at the look of indignation on Inge's face. "They did not want to know us, either."

Chapter 17

"Then why did they come today, such a long way?"

"They wanted money. They need money to buy food." Frau Landmann pushed away her half-eaten slice of bread. "They came to me as a...as a last resort."

"The poor child....Did you give them any?" Inge was prepared to hear a scoffing denial, but her grandmother nodded.

"Not much, though," she said. "It'll get them home, but not much more." She laid her hands palms up on the table and added, "You see, we don't have much ourselves, now."

Inge had suspected that. When she went shopping, Oma gave her very little cash and instructed her in detail on the amounts to spend for the various purchases. They now used laundry soap for toilet purposes, and there were no more eggs to slap into Oma's skin.

"It'll be better once the house is sold. We'll have some money then." Frau Landmann tried to sound cheerful.

"But where will we live, afterwards?"

"You'll be in Belgium by then, with your parents. And I...I have been thinking. I think I would like to go to Hamburg, to be near my sister there."

Inge knew her great-aunt Ottilie only slightly. She was a small birdlike woman, white-haired, and the only features that marked her and Frau Landmann as sisters, were the high forehead and strong straight mouth. In great-aunt Ottilie's face, that mouth was curiously out of proportion. She was married to a civil servant, long since retired. The couple had always lived in Hamburg. Inge had never visited there, had met them only at her grandmother's house. They had one daughter, now in Venezuela with her family. Maybe it would be a good idea for Oma to go to Hamburg. At least she would not be alone, until she could join Inge's parents in Belgium.

Inge could not bear the thought of leaving Oma, and the house. Oma was her reality, her here-and-now, warm-bodied, big, dispensing security. Inge's parents in Belgium were a mere memory, and a future unknown. What proof did she even have of their existence? A few letters? No, Oma was her home. She had drifted off in her thoughts, when Frau Landmann recalled her abruptly to the present.

"I want you to deliver a note at Herr Flasche's house, tomorrow on your way to the village." It was said in a tone that allowed no refusal. Nevertheless, Inge rebelled.

"Those people! I don't ever want to see them again!" She hammered a fist on the table in a miniature copy of one of her grandmother's gestures. The old lady grinned in recognition.

"You'll have to swallow your pride, I'm afraid," she said. "Herr Flasche is the only person able--and willing!--to help us. And help we need, to get you out."

"I don't want to leave!"

"Let's not go through all this again. It's quite useless. I *know* that you don't want to go. What you want has nothing to do with it. Nor what I want, for that matter," she added softly, reluctantly. "Your parents have entrusted you to my care, and I intend to see to it that you reach them safely and in good health."

Chapter 17

The old lady groped for the cane that was hooked over the back of her chair, and levered herself up. She looked critically around the kitchen where they now ate, to save unnecessary work.

"This place is getting depressingly filthy," she remarked.

Inge felt a twinge of guilt. "I'll do some cleaning now, Oma," she said. "You go and have your rest. Go lie down."

"I think I will, child. I'm feeling the cold in my old bones."

Inge listened to her grandmother's slow progress up the stairs. She stopped, groaning, at every step. At last, the door closed on the sound of her dragging footsteps, and Inge set to work.

She had been neglecting the household chores. She saw no point in keeping the house in a good condition for buyers whom she regarded as usurpers. Consequently, she spent much of her time curled up in the library, devouring novels far too adult for her. But she lost herself in them, and that, to Inge, was time well spent. After all, there was nowhere to go, nothing exciting to do. The walks in the forest that she loved above all in the fall, were now forbidden. German forests were out of bounds to Jews.

And there was no one to see. The small Jewish community of the town had dispersed. Those who had the possibility, had emigrated. Others had joined relatives in larger communities in near-by cities. Some had been sent to concentration camps.

Frau Grünberg and Hannelore had disappeared, no one knew where. Her daughter and son-in-law had been quietly buried in the Jewish cemetery. A few days after the funeral, their graves had been found trampled, and swastikas of white paint poured onto the leveled ground. Frau Grünberg was not there to know about it. Her old friend saw to it that the graves were cleaned up and decent markers set on them.

The few Gentiles who had until then remained Frau Landmann's acknowledged friends, now stayed away. Irmgard Lumpe had come one day to visit Inge.

She alone of all the people who had been close to her, had the courage to be seen in broad daylight in a Jewish home. But Inge was entangled in a net of mistrust, and she suspected her friend of sly curiosity. She had received Irmgard coldly, and Irmgard had not come back.

After the visit, Inge regretted bitterly that she had rejected the one hand extended to her in friendship.

The day after the poor relations' visit, Inge waited to go down the hill until the middle of the morning, when she knew few people would be about. It cost her a great effort to walk up the worn steps to the slate house and push the envelope with Herr Flasche's name on it, under the front door. She rang the bell and ran, hiding behind the hedge in the bend of the road. From there, she could observe the green door. She waited until it was opened by Frau Flasche who looked more untidy than ever. The woman peered at the letter shortsightedly, turned it over, then slipped it into her apron pocket. She looked around a moment to see who had delivered it then, seeing no one, she went inside again and closed the door. Inge continued down the hill.

Chapter 17

Late that afternoon, it started to rain. It was bitter cold and soon the rain turned to sleet. There was no comfort in the house. It smelled of damp and cold ashes, and breath steamed out of Inge's nostrils. She wrapped herself in sweaters and retired to the library where, because she had been forbidden to read him, she tried to lose herself in a novel by Gabriele d'Annunzio. She found him incomprehensible and boring, and wondered why she was not allowed to read him.

She had left her grandmother in the dining room, poring over a casket full of jewelry. This had obviously not been kept in the bedroom safe, since it still existed after the raid. Inge herself was bored by the glittering things and did not wonder why Frau Landmann had got them out.

She was sent to bed soon after supper. "It's the best place to keep warm," her grandmother told her.

Once during the night, Inge woke up. She heard muffled voices, a man's and her grandmother's, nearly as deep. Then the sound dimmed and Inge drifted back into sleep. By morning, she had forgotten about it. It was Frau Landmann's unusual silence at breakfast that recalled the incident to her mind.

"Oma," she asked, "who was here last night?"

The old lady gazed at Inge over her spectacles. "What makes you think anyone was here?"

"I woke up and heard voices. Yours, and a man's."

"You may as well know. That letter you delivered yesterday, it was to summon Herr Flasche to the house."

"And he came, just like that? Because you asked him? Wasn't he ashamed?"

"He stood to gain by it," Frau Landmann said. "*If* he cared to take the risk. Remember, it was he who suggested it in the first place."

In a flash, Inge now recalled the jewelry. "Did you *give* him something?" she demanded. "After what he has taken already?"

"Let's be fair, child." The old lady flushed painfully. "You know as well as I that it is highly unlikely that *he* took your platinum. In fact, I am sure that he did not. It was that good-for-nothing son of his."

"Did he say so? Did he mention him at all, *or* Elfriede?"

"Of course he made no mention of the looting. He probably does not even know about that. I asked after his children. He said the girl had a cold, and that he doesn't know about that Willi." Frau Landmann glanced at Inge and a triumphant smile flickered over her face. "It seems he disappeared on the night we were taken to jail."

"He hasn't come back?"

Frau Landmann shook her head. "Nor has he given any sign of life," she said.

"Did you tell Herr Flasche about the theft, and about my doll?" Inge asked.

Frau Landmann shrugged. "No, I did not. There really was no point in saying anything. He couldn't do anything about it if he wanted to, with things as they are."

Both relapsed into silence. Inge was burning to know what her grandmother and Herr Flasche had arranged between them. Yet she was fearful, as knowledge meant the end of uncertainty, and she was not at all sure that she did not prefer to believe life might continue as it was. Frau Landmann obviously did not want to enlighten her at this time, and presently, with a deep sigh, the old lady left the table and made her way slowly up the stairs. Inge cleared away the dishes and washed them.

Each time that morning that Inge met her grandmother, the old lady put on a show of busyness that allowed no interruption. Over the midday meal--bouillon made from soup cubes, boiled potatoes and pickled herrings--the two avoided eye contact. Finally, Inge could not bear the strain any longer.

"Oma, what *did* you arrange with Herr Flasche?" she burst out.

Frau Landmann let out a resigned sigh. "Nothing, as yet," she said. "I asked him to make inquiries." Absently she mashed a potato with her fork. "He'll let me know as soon as he has made some contacts." She laid the fork down and pushed away her plate. "You can finish it. I'm not hungry."

Inge did not have to be told twice. These days, her appetite was never satisfied. She wolfed down any food that she could find; nothing went to waste.

By evening, they had heard nothing from Herr Flasche yet. Nor did they hear anything in the days that followed. Inge amused herself by drawing pictures on the windowpanes in the film made by her breath.

At the end of the month, a buyer turned up for the house. He was the owner of a department store in town, where Frau Landmann had been a long-time customer in better days. This was an opportunity for the merchant to move to a more exclusive neighborhood. He paid the price the assessors had determined. Frau Landmann shrugged. She no longer cared.

She engaged a removal firm to crate and store as many of her belongings as she was allowed to keep. The rest she sold to the new owner, together with the Oriental rugs. He thought they gave the house the desired *cachet*. He got them at bargain prices, as he did the fittings and draperies. Inge wondered if he was really going to fumigate the house.

She furiously pulled all the books from the shelves in the library and heaped them in the middle of the floor. She threw herself on the top of the pile, buried her arms in the books and cried for her loss. Tears, mixed with the dust of years, streaked her face.

Frau Landmann sewed a rectangular pocket into the lining of Inge's winter coat, stuffed it with an envelope full of folded sheets of rare postage stamps, and sewed it up securely.

"These should help a little, over there," she said. "Make sure you give them to your father straight away. He'll know what to do with them. I converted what I could into these stamps. They are valuable."

Inge felt their stiffness crackle against her stomach when she slipped on the coat. It's like the platinum all over again, she thought, and I hope that I won't ruin it all this time! She had no curiosity to see the stamps. In fact, she had lost interest in most things. Apathy clung to her like enshrouding cobwebs.

Upon instructions from her grandmother, Inge gathered together her walking boots, warm snow pants, a

Chapter 17

couple of sweaters and the coat, and piled them in a heap at the foot of her bed. When the call finally came, she was to be ready at a moment's notice.

On the night of December third, Herr Flasche came for her. She did not know until then that the time had come. Oma had given her no warning. What self-control this meant for the old lady, Inge realized only years later. There was time only for a frantic embrace. Inge's eyes were blurred and she did not see her grandmother's face clearly. She had an impression of reaching arms, and then Herr Flasche made her lie down on flattened sacks on the floor of a car and covered her from head to foot with a scratchy blanket.

As they drove off, Inge felt her bond with her grandmother stretch and tighten until she thought that it might break with a twang and slam back into her heart. But it held, it held. She was at the end of her capacity to react, and so exhausted that her head buzzed. The pain of it, combined with the steady purr of the engine and the pervading cold, numbed her into an uneasy sleep. Later, she could only recall vaguely what followed, but isolated patches of sharpness were etched indelibly into her dreamlike awareness.

She remembered a warm farm kitchen where a kind-faced woman made her eat a bowlful of thick pea soup with pieces of bacon floating in it, and bread. She had stroked Inge's head, murmuring, "Poor child, poor child."

Inge nearly wept then.

Herr Flasche had disappeared, she could not remember when. Then a man in a flat cap led her by the hand through dark meadows, lifted for her barbed-wire fences under which she was made to crawl. Inge remembered the crunch of frosty grass under her boots, and the sharp smell of the night. She remembered how later, she stood breathlessly still while a patrol of German border guards marched metallically down a hard road between pine forests. When she tired, the man carried her on his shoulders. Inge remembered her bone-weariness, and the numbing cold, and the silence.

At one point, another man joined them quietly. One of them carried Inge over a stream, and water gurgled against his thighs. And once they froze--forever, it seemed--in the beam of a searchlight. It impaled them helpless on the spear of its light, then mercifully groped further into the darkness, leaving them able to breathe again.

Inge did not know at what point they crossed the border into Belgium, but when at last, fully clothed, she was laid down in a high feather bed, she knew that she had made it, and slept.

In the morning, her hosts, a plump German-speaking couple, gave her a breakfast of fresh crusty rolls with butter and honey, and a cup of warm milky coffee, then they put her on the train in Eupen, a little town near the border. They warned her not to talk to anyone. Around midday, she arrived in Brussels, at the Gare du Nord. An odor of fried food floated insistently around the station, and Inge felt nauseated.

Her father met her on the platform. He was a grayer, thinner man than she remembered. He wept as he swept her into his arms. Inge was embarrassed at this display of emotion by a virtual stranger. His glasses had steamed

Chapter 17

up. She pushed him away.

"Where is my mother?" she asked, her throat tight.

Herr Richter pressed his lips together at Inge's aloofness. He grasped her shoulder and steered her towards the exit. "She's waiting in the taxi," he said. He stopped, took both Inge's hands in his. "I want you to be gentle when you meet her. She is still in pain from her broken leg."

Inge withdrew her hands. She felt icy from head to foot, and showed no pleasure at the reunion. Her father looked at her with yearning eyes.

"Well?" he said.

Inge's gaze slid sideways, away from his face. She noted without interest the people milling about so freely, so warmly dressed and busy and well-fed. What is Oma doing now, she wondered, where is Oma?

A long time ago, I was looking forward to coming here, she thought. But now, I only want to be home, with Oma.

She was afraid of this man beside her, this stranger, and of the woman in the taxi.

Herr Richter drew a deep breath and gave Inge a little shake. He forced a smile to his lips.

"Come now, Inge," he said. "Mutti is waiting."

POSTSCRIPT

Emma Landmann, my grandmother, died in December, 1939, at the age of seventy-six. Not long before her death, we had received a letter from her, postmarked Hamburg. She had moved there after leaving her hometown, to be near her only remaining close relative in Germany, her sister Ottilie.

Oma's handwriting had become spidery, barely legible. She had sold the typewriter that in the last few years had enabled the recipients of her letters to read them.

"I see Ottilie every day," she had written. "She has grown old and feeble, it's a shame. I managed to rent a little room, light and airy. There's a lovely view from the window." And then she quoted her favorite verse from the quintessential German poet, Johann Wolfgang von Goethe:

> "... Allen Gewalten zum Trotz sich erhalten,
> Nimmer sich beugen, kräftig sich zeigen,
> Rufet die Arme der Götter herbei."*

One week after Oma's letter, we received one from my great-aunt Ottilie. She informed us that her sister had died three days before. My grandmother had refused to move in with her sister and brother-in-law, preferring to the end to 'defy all tyrants' alone.

As a Jew, Oma had had difficulties in obtaining lodgings. All she had been able to find, in spite of her still relatively ample means, was an unheated attic room "with a lovely view," five floors up in a tenement. It had no running water. Oma had died on the stairs, carrying a pail of water up from a landing three floors below.

---

*   Free translation:
   "...Defying all tyrants, you will survive,
   Never submit, but show your strength
   This will ensure you the help of the gods."

ABOUT MARGOT GRÜNEWALD MASSEY

The author was born in 1926 in Germany, the youngest child in a prosperous middle-class Jewish family. Her parents went ahead to Belgium in 1937, leaving Margot behind with her grandmother. In the spring of 1939, her mother came back for her, and the two made an illegal escape into Belgium. *Spring into Winter* is loosely based on these experiences. In 1942, Margot and her two siblings, under different names, were hidden in a castle--a period to be covered in Ms. Massey's next book. All three children survived the war. Their parents were deported to Auschwitz in May 1943; they did not return.